Witness 87

Is she truly free?

Rosie Elliot

Copyright © 2022 Rosie Elliot
All rights reserved.
No part of this publication may be reproduced,
stored or transmitted, in any form or by any means,
electronic, mechanical, photocopying or otherwise,
without the prior written permission of the author.
The right of R Elliot to be identified as the Author
of this work has been asserted by her in accordance
with the Copyright, Designs and Patents Act of
1988.

This is a work of fiction. Names, places, events and
incidents are either the products of the author's
imagination or have been used fictitiously.
Any resemblance to any person living or deceased
is purely coincidental.

A CIP catalogue record for this book is available
from the British Library.

ISBN: 979-8-4085-7582-4
Also available as an eBook

DEDICATION

To all those who have suffered,
and are suffering still.

ACKNOWLEDGMENTS

Simon Drysdale, my partner in life;
Ann Uddin (member of the Pevensey Plungers swimming community) for her wonderful cover photo;
George Wicker Copywriting Services for cover design and technical skills
David Nance for his constructive feedback

PROLOGUE

Oh my! It's SO good to be free! I don't have an enormous number of regrets because I knew it was right. At the time.

My baptism at fifteen was expected. By mum, by the elders, by the friends I'd made. I didn't feel too young and I knew exactly what I was getting myself into. The Christian principles and the Organisation's rules were clear: why delay dedicating my life to God? If I knew the Truth then the sooner I got baptised and made that public declaration of faith then the sooner I would come under God's protection. By getting baptised I would be saved when Armageddon comes - when God destroys all the wicked people. I had no doubts whatsoever that I was doing the right thing. I loved God and this was the most natural thing to do.

Dad wasn't there to see me being dunked in the local swimming pool. He'd had enough of mum's obsession; this new religion that had been brought to her by two seventeen-year-old girls selling their magazines. He'd got out, and taken my half-sisters with him leaving myself, mum and my brother Peter. Mum was then free to devote her life to studying, attending meetings and going door to door preaching to people, spreading the good news of God's Kingdom, soon to rule over the earth. I think she was secretly relieved that dad had gone.

Mum was genuine but clearly unbalanced. It wasn't good for a small child's head to be filled with pictures of people running from fireballs falling from heaven at Armageddon, or to learn that the devil will make a target of her because she is on God's side. It was the stuff of nightmares.

I was a good girl, obedient and did 'the Truth' very well, judging by the comments from others. My progression and spiritual maturity were noticed in the answers I gave during the Watchtower study and the Tuesday Book study, the talks I gave on the platform and in my ministry. But I soon began to find it monotonous and severely lacking in the kind of excitement a youngster needed. Hobbies, youth clubs, after school groups, none of which was allowed. That left a congregation barn dance every couple of months and maybe a walk round the lake. Boring.

By sixteen, a year after my baptism I'd had enough and fell right off the tracks. What had I done? What a lot of teenagers do; fell for the charms of a teenage boy that I wasn't married to, bringing shame to myself, to my family, to the congregation and to God. We'd met on the campsite that myself and several other Witnesses were staying at for the summer JW convention in Norwich. This non-Witness boy had bought me a lager and made eyes at me across the pool table in the clubhouse. The little bit of attention he gave me was enough to turn my head and the excitement was too much. I needed more of what he was offering; Ray was someone new, he had different things to talk about, a view of life I'd not come across before. In such contrast to my boring Witness life. Ray seemed normal – not at all like the boys in the congregation who were purely ministry-minded and nothing else. I had to go for it, had to leave before I died of boredom.

A few days after I'd arrived back home from the convention, I caught the bus straight back out to Norwich, back to Ray at the campsite, and we became an item. But no sooner had we done the deed in his tent - with his brother banished to the clubhouse for a while - than my scripturally-trained conscience kicked in. With the realisation of what I'd done, I felt as if I'd been booted in the stomach and knew I was right in line to be disfellowshipped. Good morals were expected and checked up on within the congregation. It always felt as if I couldn't even stand and talk to a young Brother without it being remarked upon. There was no such thing as a platonic relationship. That kind of friendship couldn't possibly exist in the Truth. I really didn't know how young couples got together and built a successful relationship, being watched all the time.

But, for some reason I couldn't leave Ray. I was too scared to face up to what I'd done. None of it had been planned – earning our money fruit-picking, having to move on when the season finished, arriving on the south coast and knocking on mum's Witness friend, Kathy's, door. We'd just gone with the flow, did what we needed to do to survive and pay our way. Once in Eastbourne, Ray was sat down and given a weekly Bible study with Kathy's husband, Greg. There was no argument. We had dumped ourselves on them and put them in a very difficult position, that was true. They could have turned us away, or me at least – I was the one that was baptised, committed to living a moral life. Now I'd ruined it and they could have sent me packing.

Ray and I got jobs at the local Beefeater Steak House down the road, Ray behind the bar and me waitressing. I couldn't face going to any meetings and thankfully, Kathy didn't push me. I wouldn't have been able to look anyone in the face – they would have known what I'd been up to as soon as I'd made eye contact. My conscience was killing me and the guilt was oozing out of every pore. I knew I would have to go back home at some point and confess my sin, and the catalyst for that was my dad.

Mum had been trying to find out where I was as I hadn't told her when I'd left, just upped and disappeared, balancing a note against the clock for her to find. She must have kept dad's number as she called him and told him what I'd been up to. He phoned me at Kathy's and told me to leave my job, leave Eastbourne and go up to his place in Uxbridge. He gave me a right telling off.

This was the first time I'd seen him since the age of 8 – half my life ago. I found it funny that he was having a go at me. What right had he got? He'd cleared off out of my life, why would he start caring about me now? Anyway, I stayed at his for a few days and then he took me back home to mum in the Midlands with my tail between my legs.

My confession came quickly, I had to get this sorted out. My Judicial Committee meeting with those three Elders at the Kingdom Hall was an experience I'll never forget. My life changed forever that night. I was alone, mum couldn't face coming along to support me. After the intensity and the disgusting depth of their questioning they decided I needed to be disfellowshipped. The news cut me to the heart as I'd been led to believe that God would have mercy on those who confess their sins. Not so, according to these three. I was considered to be insufficiently repentant because I stayed with Ray – I hadn't immediately left the scene of my spiritual crime. I should have acted like Joseph in the Bible when Potiphar's wife tried to seduce him. He scarpered straight away. But I guess he wasn't in a tent out on the east coast, in the middle of the night with no money and no means of transport.

So, I had no choice but to take my punishment, and try not to spend my days in tears at having lost my friends and what little family I had left, overnight. The announcement was short, but not particularly sweet: "Jessica Dalton is no longer one of Jehovah's Witnesses." That's all that was needed. The congregation then knew how to treat me – no interaction on any level, and, as the Bible instructed, "not even offering a greeting." That was the Governing Body's interpretation anyway. Everyone was very obedient. It seemed that some took particular delight in crossing over the road to avoid me.

As a deep depression attacked me hard I knew that the only way to get out of my situation was to get back into the Truth, back into the warmth of this loving congregation I belonged to. I kept going to the meetings, sitting on the back row, arriving just before the first song and departing just after the final prayer, in silence, alone. That was a long year, at the end of which my application to be reinstated was accepted. I genuinely wanted to get back. It was the only right way to live; surrounded by a loving, caring, spiritual family of Brothers and Sisters. Each one would be prepared to die for me. Where would I find that kind of love out in the world? In the Truth was where I belonged.

Now I could start my life again. My attempts to put the past behind me worked well, for a while. Immersing myself in spiritual activities: meeting preparation; arranging in advance who to work with on the ministry; re-joining the Ministry School and giving role-play talks on the platform; doing demonstrations. It was all such important stuff – spiritual education directly from the Governing Body in New York. My head was full of nothing but the Truth. Yes, this was the 'real life' and I was so blessed to know the Truth about God and the universe. I knew things that the rest of the world didn't, and it was my responsibility to tell them, warn them about Armageddon. I was back to having purpose, structure and security in my life again.

But it didn't last. There was no fun, no excitement and nothing to look forward to except putting my ministry report in or booking the coach for the coming assembly. Life was quickly becoming monotonous and boring for a teenage girl once again.

Everything revolved around the religion – what I wore (no skirts above the calves and no low necklines); where I went (no pubs unless in a large group, be choosy about which films to see at the cinema); who I mixed with (only Witness friends were allowed), what I drank (watch that alcohol); what I ate (no blood products); how I looked (not too much make up otherwise you'll look like a prostitute, no tattoos and only one ear piercing); where I worked (nowhere that conflicts with Christian values, i.e. a pub, gambling establishment, cigarette factory, the military). There was no escape. No chance to breathe.

But it wasn't quite the same as before. Previous friends, or those I thought were my friends, were now keeping themselves at arm's length. That's because I was damaged goods, bad association, someone to be cautious of, lest they be influenced by my independent way of thinking. Forgiveness was a subject that wasn't given that much attention in the magazines, except when it came to God himself. He was forgiving, I believed that. But as for the congregation, well, I never truly felt it. And it was clear to see that when it came to congregation outings they'd certainly never forgotten my appalling behaviour. I would usually find out about them after the event. The ostracism remained and was keeping me in a semi-permanent state of depression.

So, once again, I felt desperate to get out. But I did it properly this time. During the time I'd been at Kathy's with Ray some regular customers at the Beefeater – the mother, Esther, and her son, Will - had helped me out one evening when I'd had a panic attack at work. We'd stayed in touch and had become good friends despite my having been raised to reject friendship with anyone in the 'world'. I could see they were different, genuine and unrestricted in their kindness.

Esther was just so lovely and a good listener. She asked me gently about my life and made me feel safe about opening up and I explained everything that had happened. I didn't know if I could make her understand the Witness mentality but I found her and Will to be completely non-judgemental and accepting of me for who I was. When I was in their company I felt free to be me, not continually watching myself as I knew many in the congregation were.

Esther made me an offer of a room in her house by the sea and I grabbed it with both hands. I went to live with her in Pevensey Bay about a year ago. It has been wonderful! Of course, I miss mum, but I speak to her regularly. Peter has decided to be loyal to the Organisation and doesn't want that much to do with me anymore because I've rejected Jehovah. But sadly that means I don't get to see my little niece, Bethany. That breaks my heart, but I had to weigh things up. It's Peter's choice to reject me just as it was the choice of all those in the congregation to ostracise me for a whole year. They didn't have to. They could have broken the rules and had lunch with me, but no. If they'd been caught and reported to the Elders they would have been in line for some serious shunning themselves.

The practice of shunning killed my friend Alan. Turned out he was as gay as a May pole, which is a complete no no in the Truth. I asked myself if the Elders realised that their actions had contributed to his death? Did they know that by disfellowshipping him how desperate they had made him feel? The thought of losing his whole family and all his friends was too much for him to bear and, if he was truly gay, then he was as good as dead anyway, in their eyes. But, of course, the view of the Witnesses was that Alan only had himself to blame. It was his own actions that got him kicked out, he knew what the rules were and he just shouldn't have gone down that road. After he died, I felt in my heart that God could not approve of such actions by the Elders, that their interpretation of those scriptures instructing shunning was wrong. It had to be; it was inhumane. And as for him being a homosexual, well, that was a whole different subject that I couldn't begin to understand. But there must have been some kind of support for him from somewhere, surely. Some way that he could have found happiness. Now his poor parents think they'll never see him again because it was suicide. There's no comfort for them. No hope. But for some reason they still go to the meetings.

My guilt about my wrongdoing has eased as time's gone by and I've been able to get it into perspective, get my head around the injustice of my treatment, put it in its place. It still jumps up from time to time and trips me up and I end up feeling sorry for myself for a few days. But then it passes and I carry on. Usually.

This past year or so has been an eye opener to the world around me. A world that I didn't know existed. For instance, I've seen how family members interact with one another when they're not stressed out and under pressure to perform on the ministry or the platform. Genuine friends that fall out with one another, have a blazing row to clear the air and then make up again. Rows? Shouting? Anger in the Truth? No, everything is done with a quiet and mild spirit, everything is under control. Out there kids are allowed to be kids. They're not made to sit still in silence for hours at the meetings. They're not exposed to nastiness at people's front doors. I've seen a normal world and I like it.

It's spring 1987 and I'm into the last of my teenage years. I live away from home, I'm independent and I'm free. Free to wear what I want, eat what I want, mix with whoever I chose. I can celebrate Christmas, eat chocolate eggs at easter, get dressed up at Halloween. I can send mystery Valentine's cards, connect with my Irish roots on St Patrick's Day. If I feel like it, I can stand in respect to Her Majesty when the National Anthem is played, I can wave the British flag, I can vote in the next election, I can go to college and learn a skill. Work full-time! Make new friends who don't judge me.

I feel as free as a bird! Now, I can do anything I want.

CHAPTER 1

Every time I moved my head I felt a sharp pain across the nape of my neck. Some of my hair had got caught up in the knot of the blindfold. I resolved to keep it as still as I could. The two guides at my side pushed me forward and underfoot I could feel the flooring change from carpet to wood. I trod cautiously as I was manoeuvred, holding my arms out ahead for balance. I heard whispers; unfamiliar voices; a loud pop! sounded to my right, making me jump.

The volume of the voices increased as I continued my secret journey, tentatively placing one foot in front of the other not know where I was heading. They stopped me and held my upper arms. A hush descended and I wondered what was going to happen next.

I had never heard the song in such close quarters before. The joyfulness of the simple tune sung a zillion times since its composer laid the bars down. The intimacy of the words rang out as my blindfold was removed. After the darkness of the preceding few minutes, the brightness made me squint and I couldn't help but giggle as I took in the scene before me.

I saw the faces. Beaming, happy faces all looking expectantly at me, their lips moving in sync. Someone had thrown in some harmonies. It was beautiful! A long pause occurred just after my own name was sung and before the final line and then came cheers and applause. I didn't know what to look at, or who, or where.

Will. Where's Will? From somewhere off to my left he came and stood by my side, smiling with his dark eyes as well as his lips, and wrapped his arm around my waist. I knew I was beaming from ear to ear but suddenly I felt the urge to burst out laughing. Then Will was laughing and then everyone else joined in. But I didn't know what should have happened next. The song had finished. I looked to Will to guide me. Everyone was just staring at me and smiling. *What am I supposed to do? Should I say something?*

Thankfully the voices jumped in to save me from my dilemma. "Jess! Happy birthday darling," "……birthday, Jess…" "hey, have a good one….." "…Surprise!.." All these voices, all at the same time! Mark, my boss at the Beefeater Steak House, where all this was taking place, put a glass of bubbly pink liquid in my hand and Will then led me over to a table by the window, its surface piled with wrapped presents adorned with colourful bows and tags. I could see the scattering of envelopes all bore my name. *Are these really all for me?* I couldn't believe my eyes and thought for a second I was dreaming, that this was all for somebody else and I'd just got sucked into it.

"Thought we'd surprise you! The look on your face!!" I vaguely heard Will's voice, as if coming towards me through a tunnel. I couldn't speak. I stared at the table laden with gifts, cards, colour, sandwiches, crisps, a huge chocolate cake with candles stuck in the top, plastic cups, paper plates. Balloons bounced around tied to the table legs, a huge banner flew above stating, "HAPPY BIRTHDAY JESSICA." I'd never seen the restaurant looking like this before. I wondered why Mark and Jane had asked me to come in early at ten for the afternoon shift. Now I know.

Out of nowhere some music started up: Chic's 'Le Freak', a classic that Will knew I loved. How anyone could sit still when this came on, I don't know. He'd been responsible for all this, I was sure. The dark horse. How could he not tell me? I would have worn something more appropriate, not my work uniform. My hair! I would have done my hair nicely and put some more make-up on, and lipstick. Heels! I could have worn heels. I wish he'd told me! I must have looked a right mess.

All the tables and chairs in the restaurant extension had been pushed back against the wall and the dozen or so guests were dancing on the small wooden square of floor in the middle. They were chatting to each other, moving around, laughing. Among the other faces I recognised was Will's older brother Duncan, down for a break from Manchester where he worked as a newly qualified doctor. Esther's younger sister, Gail; Theresa one of the lifeguards from the swimming pool and Neil her boyfriend.

Theresa and Neil had been so helpful when I'd first arrived a year ago. Swimming was a passion of mine and I wanted to put my skills to good use. One day after a rather strenuous session in the pool I decided to enquire about lifeguard training. I didn't really know how to find out about such a thing so, as Theresa had always been friendly, I sought her out and put the question to her. At the end of her shift she'd sat down with me in the café and, over a cup of tea, had informed me about the options available. She really knew her stuff. The courses on offer were expensive and I wasn't sure I could fit it around my job at the Beefeater but it certainly gave me something to think about. We chatted frequently at the pool after that, and Theresa and her boyfriend always spoke to me when they came in the restaurant.

Mark came over to me and explained that Laura and Danny, who ran the bar, were responsible for all the decorations and Stuart the chef brought over the CDs that Will had requested. He said Sandy and Ellie (two Friday night regulars that I'd come to know) should be here any minute. There were some good people who worked and ate at the Beefeater.

Mark and his wife Jane had been so kind to let me have my old job back. Especially as I'd left without giving any notice. They could have laughed in my face when I went up there on my return to Eastbourne to see if they had any vacancies. But instead, they said that some of the customers had been asking where I was and when I was coming back so were happy to give me some regular shifts again. I was so lucky. Lucky, or blessed? I still don't know about that one.

Through the door to the extension burst Sandy and Ellie, arm in arm. They always made quite an entrance and today was no different. Sandy did some kind of dance thing with a twirl at the end and finished up directly in front of me presenting a gorgeous bunch of flowers. Ellie bobbed around to the disco beat and shouted to acting DJ Stuart to put on some Erasure. Disco was *so* over, man!

I stood still. Looking at the table. Looking around me. Looking at Will. Not one fibre of my being had known about this, it was a complete surprise and there was just so much to take in. I had never celebrated my birthday growing up in the Witness faith and I'd certainly never been to anyone else's birthday party. It just wasn't done. Their reasons for not observing someone's arrival on the planet were based on terrible birthday experiences recorded in the Bible and involved heads being cut off and we wouldn't want that to happen, would we? So, no birthdays. That's how it was. I'd never felt left out, not really, well, maybe a couple of times when girls at school showed me what their parents had bought them for their 13th or whatever. But it was the presents I was envious of, not the party.

This was a whole new thing for me and I wasn't sure how to proceed. The suspense of the blindfold, the curiosity of being manhandled and pushed in a particular direction, the surprise of it all and a group of people all looking at me and singing…. to me. It was too much to take in and I felt my heart starting to beat faster. Then my breaths started to get shorter. An increasingly familiar feeling of panic erupted and suddenly I had to go, had to get myself away from this!

I ran from the fold of Will's arm back through the doorway and straight into the ladies' toilets. This was just too much. It was embarrassing! All right, I turned It a couple of weeks ago. It's not worth celebrating now, it's too late! What's the point if the moment has passed? I don't get it. And all those cards and presents! It's too much for one person. It's almost obscene.

I was hot with embarrassment and nervousness and I could feel my heart pounding in my chest. The tiled wall in the ladies' felt cool on my back as I leaned against it, and I knew I just needed a few minutes to calm down. The door opened and banged on the springy wall protector at floor level, making a pinging noise. Esther, Will's mum, my lovely Esther, came towards me with arms outstretched, chuckling and shaking her head.

"Oh, Jess, what have we done to you?! Come here." She gave me one of her mother hugs, as I call them, and then held my face in her hands. Will was so lucky to have such an affectionate mother. "Take a deep breath or two, in, hold, and out, that's right." She was a nurse and knew what to do with me. "When you're ready we'll go back out. It's time to open your cards. Open them one by one and if the person is in the room, just go over to them and say 'thankyou.' Same with the presents. Do you want me to stay with you?"

"Yes please, Esther, I'm not sure about all this. It's been more of a shock than a surprise." She checked my face and, seeing there were no tears and no mascara tracks running down to my chin, we set off to do as she'd instructed. She stayed by my side while I thanked everyone and, as I began to relax again, she allowed me some space and went to mingle with the others. But I knew she was still keeping an eye on me. That was Esther.

I soon found my feet, bobbed along to the music, Rick Astley, Pet Shop Boys, Madonna - some really groovy tunes. The glass of bubbly given to me earlier I now knocked back which gave me the confidence to throw a few shapes (is that what they call it?) on the dance floor. I was actually starting to enjoy it. It was early in the day for such lively activities, but no one seemed to care. Theresa, standing nibbling at the food on her paper plate while Neil refilled his glass, beckoned me over.

"You know, when you're in a better position and you can do your lifeguard's course, there'll more than likely be plenty of work for you at the Leisure Pool. Or you could go freelance and that leaves you free to work anywhere."

I perched myself on the edge of a chair piled with coats and bags and listened intently as she told me more facts about the job she loved.

She was a stable person, had been doing the job for several years and kept herself fit and strong. She had given me good advice. There was so much I had yet to learn about the way things worked out there in the big, wide, worldly world: employment, paying tax and national Insurance, courses, funding, apprenticeships etc. I didn't even know what I didn't know.

None of this was taught in my school. And as for learning anything valuable from my mum, well, she kind of left it to the Elders – anything I needed to know they would tell me from the platform or it would turn up in either the Watchtower of the Awake magazine. Work was a somewhat dirty word amongst the Witnesses. It was never viewed as a way of making personal progress or a way to develop valuable skills or self-worth. It was simply a means to survive. The encouragement from the religion was that, on leaving school, all the young ones would only need to work part time doing a low-pressure job, such as cleaning windows or filing in an office, so that they would have time to pioneer. A commitment to spend at least sixty hours a month preaching the Good News to members of the public should not be taken lightly and once your completed form was submitted you were tied. Work? It wasn't that important. Not as important as preaching.

But one activity that was important to me was swimming. I'm sure it was in my blood. I loved it. So now I was becoming independent I wondered if I could take it further. My sister, Diane, had been the one out of my three sisters who had taught me to swim. She was the one whose patience had paid off when I completed my first width, and then my first length. She had been so proud of me and bought me a pair of goggles with her first week's wages from her job at Sainsbury's. Then she left. They all left. Dad (Ben), Karen, Jackie and Diane. Half my family disappeared literally overnight.

And now I'm supposed to be working a lunchtime shift but instead I'm drinking wine and dancing and opening presents and cards and laughing with friends and strangers and my boss and my boyfriend in my awful work uniform.

"Will, hey Will, come here! Come and dance with me, Will, you need to dance with me," and grabbing his T shirt I pulled him along. "I've got to go to work soon. I don't want to." I laid my head on his chest and felt the music wash over me as we swayed together.

My head was spinning after the small glass of wine. Witnesses weren't supposed to drink too much. There were a lot of things they weren't supposed to do but I could see them, sneaking around the wine aisles at Tesco. Hypocritical bastards, the lot of 'em. And they have the cheek to point the finger at me!! I could tell those Elders some stories. There would be a stack of disfellowshippings if I told them what I know.

"Will, don't make me go to work," I mumbled.

"Mark's given you the day off. Mum's making a nice meal later on, then you and I are going out tonight." I think I heard him correctly. He was tall and his voice was far so above my ears.

"Going out? Where? I need to get changed and do my hair."

"There's time for all that, just enjoy yourself right now and I'll explain later."

I felt so dizzy. I was dancing and had no idea what I looked like, but I didn't actually care. I could feel my arms and my whole body freeing up as I let the rhythm of the music deep into my head and I danced and danced and turned and stumbled and giggled. It was wonderful to feel so free.

Suddenly I was ravenous. The sausage rolls were calling me. Then the chocolate cake which, strangely, no one had touched yet. Someone said it was for me. Another voice said I had to make a wish as I blew out the nineteen candles stuck in it. I didn't have enough puff and tried several times to get them all out. I did it in the end and obliged everyone by closing my eyes and making a secret wish. The smell of extinguished matches lingering in the air conjured vague memories of power cuts as a child and picking candle wax off a saucer.

I'm not going to say what I wished for. Maybe later…although I've been told that if you disclose it, it won't come true. What a load of rubbish! Is this what people really believe? When I think about it though, it's a nice idea, wishing something will come true. Is a wish like a prayer? Who do you direct it to? God? The air? The universe? Does it even work? Maybe it's all tied up with the genie in the lamp? I'll keep an eye on things. If it does come true, the act of wishing could prove to be a very useful tool.

I thanked Mark for laying on the buffet, pointing at him and tapping my nose. And Laura and Danny for blowing up all those balloons. Sandy and Ellie for coming along and Stuart, dressed in his chequered chef's trousers, for being a great DJ. And I told them all off for drinking wine so early on a Saturday morning. They all deserved a friendly slap on the wrist for keeping this a secret. And the presents. Well, the presents were amazing. Things I really needed and hadn't brought down with me – a hairdryer, a proper gym bag, a pair of trainers, a voucher to spend in Jean Jeanie, the denim shop in town. I couldn't believe these people had chosen such appropriate items and, again, it was possible to see Will and Esther's influence in all of this.

In that moment, saying goodbye and thankyou to everyone, I had a list of questions in my head. As I heard their voices and saw their smiles I wondered, *had all the guests been told that I'd never celebrated my birthday before? That I didn't know how a birthday party was supposed to run? That I'd been raised as a Jehovah's Witness almost from birth? Do I want everyone to know? What will they think of me? I'd suffered bullying and being singled-out throughout my school life, frequent rejection and being sworn at and spat at when I knocked at people's front doors: some even threatened to set their dogs on me. And if they did know, how will they be with me after today?* I wondered if these connections I had made in the last year would survive if they knew. Was it worth putting in the effort to make friends, real friends, only for them to find out about my past and dump me? Everything felt a little uncertain suddenly.

Sandy and Ellie bobbed over to me, glasses in hand, following the rhythm of the catchy tune being played. They gave each other a conspiratorial look before Ellie announced:

"We're taking you into town in a bit. You're in for a treat, honey bunch." Ellie did a little twirl followed by "ta da."

"What d'you mean?" I asked her. Not more treats. Not more surprises. I didn't think I could cope with any more excitement.

"Clothes shopping! Here's the deal, you have to go in the changing room and try on anything that we give you. *Anything*, ok? You need some going out clothes 'cos Will's taking you to Dixieland on the pier tonight." Ellie was so excited and kept giggling as she sipped her wine.

"What's Dixieland?" I'd never heard of it before. Was it a restaurant? Or a pub?

"It's a nightclub! You're gonna shake your little tush all night. DJ Spinney plays the best sounds and be prepared for an all-nighter. Mark and Jane will come after they finish here. There'll be loads of people down there that we know so we'll introduce you to some of them. It'll be great!"

Really? I thought to myself. *A nightclub*? The very place I had always been warned against. Nightclubs were where the Devil resides, they are full of drug-takers and knife-carriers, homosexuals and thieves. I will be dragged into their ways without even realising what's happening and then there's no going back. My relationship with God would be ruined beyond repair. No-one would want to mix with a nightclub goer. I had to think about this one and make a decision before this evening whether to go or not.

But I had to remind myself that I wasn't part of that religion any longer. I was free! Free to choose for myself what to do, wear, think, say, feel, with no-one sitting in judgement of me. But I couldn't help my instinctual reactions. The warnings I'd grown up with quickly jumped into my head and I could hear a bunch of scriptures, chapter and verse, read themselves aloud to me. Was this wise advice? Was it balanced? Would tonight be the night I start taking drugs and became a prostitute?

Should I talk to Esther about it and ask her what she thinks? She's a wise and understanding woman who I respected so much. I know she wouldn't advise me badly. But then again, at some point I've got to make up my own mind about these things.

I want to go.

I want to dance.

I want to dance all night till my feet hurt. I want to feel the beat of the deafening music pulsating through the floorboards and reaching every part of my body. I want to see a glitterball and flashing lights and hear the start of the next track playing over the end of the previous. I want to sing at the top of my voice and laugh till I'm dizzy. All night long.

In the restaurant my head was still spinning when Stuart stopped the music and people started putting on their coats. I'd only had one glass of wine, pathetic! Down the other end of the restaurant I could see the first of the lunchtime customers coming through the door and the other members of staff milling around and taking food orders. Esther approached and slipped her arm through mine.

"Happy birthday, Jessica darling. This is what you deserve. There wasn't time to organise anything for your eighteenth when you moved down last year. So Will and I thought we'd surprise you this year instead." She reached into her bag and pulled out an envelope. "Here, take this."

She stuffed it discretely into my hand telling me not to lose it. Inside there was a wad of five-pound notes. "I want you to spend this on clothes this afternoon with the girls. All of it, you hear? You'll have so much fun."

I was gobsmacked but there wasn't an opportunity to say anything, Esther detached herself from me and walked towards the door, held open by a waiting Duncan. The others were scattering, waving goodbye to me and I grabbed my jacket from the back of the chair. With Sandy and Ellie's arms through mine we made our way outside.

It felt surreal. The blue sky, the birds singing in the garden. Bags of gifts and cards in each hand, tipsy on plonk, a purse full of money – it all felt like it was happening to someone else. *I must be deep inside that dream again. How did I get here?* For the last hour and a half I'd been the centre of everybody's attention. Their eyes had been on me, my face, no-one else's. I'm not sure I liked that bit.

But I'd had a birthday party! My birth into this world, my existence, had been acknowledged, and celebrated for the very first time, damn it! Had I just arrived in the real world?

CHAPTER 2

Earlier in the day, Sandy and Ellie clearly had more fun than I did trying on clothes in town. Their sniggers reached my ears as I stood behind the curtained changing room in Debenhams. They handed me tops and skirts that I would never have looked twice at had I been shopping alone. They could see how sensibly I usually dressed. Apart from them frequenting the Beefeater, where they only saw me in my uniform, I'd been out for a couple of drinks with them in town. Jeans and a jumper was what I usually wore and, apart from that awful Beefeater dress with the ruffle neck blouse, they had never seen me in a skirt. No, and neither would they. Skirts were definitely off the menu. Ultra-smart, stuffy and shapeless was what the Sisters were made to chose from when shopping for meeting or ministry clothes. The shops just did not sell anything that ticked both smart and attractive boxes. When I attended my final meeting I swore I'd never wear a skirt again and I cut up all my meeting clothes into tiny pieces.

That was a good day. I got the feeling the girls knew that this was a whole new experience for me, but they didn't ask questions. I really respected them for that. They just accepted me as I was regardless of how I dressed.

But their hands held in front of their mouths did nothing to disguise their snorts as they threw in low-cut top after skin-tight trousers after see-through blouse. Through the curtain came dresses with long splits up the sides, a denim skirt that was, at most, a third of the length of any other skirt I'd ever worn. Tops with beads sewn in, jackets with satin collars and huge shiny black buttons linked by a chain. I was reluctant to try on these unfamiliar styles but they egged me on saying I wouldn't know how I feel unless I try them. True, I suppose. As for shoes, the range available was vast as I'd spied on the way into the shop. Some very comfortable shoes that would be great for all day on the ministry. Oh, for goodness' sake! Well, I couldn't help what came into my head, could I?

Under the gap at the bottom of the curtain Ellie threw me a pair of stilettos with what must have been a five-inch heel. They were actually, literally gorgeous. White patent with a row of tiny diamantes around the top of the heel. I squeezed my feet into them, not really believing girls actually walked from A to B in these but, at the same time, hoping I myself could manage such a feat.

With most of the items I indulged the girls by trying them on and modelling outside the fitting room. I strutted up and down like a model with hand on hip and flourishes as I turned, feeling a mixture of ridiculously stupid and quite glamorous and everything in between. We had a right laugh and so did some of the other shoppers as they looked over. But when I allowed myself a serious moment, as I peered in the full-length mirror with the curtain drawn, I had to ask: Were these clothes that exposed my legs and cleavage really so immodest, were they actually immoral? Would people look at me and think I was a right tart, that I would be an easy lay after a couple of drinks? Did this style of clothing that was designed to draw attention make me a show-off and completely worldly? And, hang on a minute, what were the girls wearing? Because if they weren't going to wear this kind of stuff then neither would I. I wasn't going to allow my lack of experience to make a fool of me.

"Ellie, what are you wearing tonight?" I wanted to see what she would choose for herself.

"I've got this top," she said pulling out a sparkly batwing number in red. "I bought it last week, it was the last one in that colour. And I'm gonna wear it with my black velvet skirt."

"Is it as short as this one?" I held up the 'belt' they'd chosen for me. Would she try to get me to wear something that she wouldn't wear herself? I wondered.

"Well, er, maybe it's slightly longer."

Right, I see. They almost got away with a little joke at my expense.

"And Sandy, what about you?"

She sniffed and shuffled about. "Black trousers and my Bowie T shirt, same as always. ''Fraid I'm not that adventurous when it comes to new clothes."

I settled for the same sparkly top as Ellie in a light blue and my determination to never wear a skirt again subsided as I spied a soft black pleather pencil skirt. It wasn't as long as I would have liked but it would just have to do. I'd never felt anything so soft.

As for the split at the back, well, I wouldn't be able to walk if it wasn't there. I'd never owned a skirt with a split in it as that was what prostitutes wore, so this was a first for me. I loved those white shoes so much I was prepared to give them a go despite the awesome height. I would practise walking in them around the house when I got home. A white clutch bag and some large white plastic button earrings completed my outfit and I felt ready to hit the town later that night.

Sandy dropped me at my front door in her Austin Metro. I manoeuvred myself out of the car with carrier bags in hand trying not to drop everything as I searched for my keys. A final reminder from Ellie about what to do with my hair was shouted from her open window:

"Just use loads of hairspray and back-comb it. You've got fluffy hair, anyway, it should look great." The car started to move away. "Oh, and make up, don't forget to slather it on otherwise there'll be no point," she shouted down the road, "and lots of mascara!" I saw the window roll up and they were gone.

I had my instructions. I had my outfit. Did I have the confidence to pull this off without making an utter fool of myself? Without doing something that showed everyone this girl has clearly never been to a nightclub before. I told myself to stop doubting. But what if I'm seen going into a nightclub? Seen? By whom? The Elders? What is an Elder going to be doing down the end of the pier on a Saturday night? They wouldn't be seen within a hundred feet of that place. Get a grip, girl.

At ten to eight and with Will for support, I toddled out to the car in my heels with my white clutch bag under my arm. *This is going to be a great night* I kept telling myself. I had to believe it.

Dixieland was the huge domed hall towards the end of Eastbourne pier. I'd walked along the wooden deck during sunny Saturday afternoons years ago, so it was familiar to me. I exited Esther's car at the entrance to the pier, trying to do so in the most modest way I knew. It would have been easier if I'd had my legs strapped together. I pulled my long-line jacket with the sleeves rolled up, around me and looked up into the night sky. It was April and dark. One or two stars were twinkling far out over the sea. The wind had picked up and now the moon was just visible through murky cloud cover. The strings of light bulbs that ran around the ticket booth and the ice cream parlour, now closed, slapped against the wooden structures, making the colours dance on the deck. I could hear the violent splashing of waves far beneath the wooden slats and I prayed the rusty Victorian structure wouldn't collapse before tonight was over.

It didn't look like anything had changed. The incredibly long walk from the street to the other end sticking out into the English Channel seemed to take forever and I teetered across the aging wooden decking hanging onto Will for fear of getting my heels stuck.

Ahead I could see the lights flashing, beckoning, all around the main entrance to Dixieland and, as someone opened the door, the indistinct sound of a heavy beat reached my ears and faded once more as the door fell shut. I couldn't wait to get on that dancefloor. The only dancing I'd carried out was at congregation weddings where some barn dance music was played. An inexperienced caller would attempt to control the groups of eight positioned in their squares but it would usually descend into chaos. It might have been enjoyable if they'd actually listened and tried to follow the instructions instead of talking and mucking about. Dancing at home in the kitchen to the Top 20 on a Sunday evening with the fluorescent tube flickering above was the nearest I'd ever got to a nightclub. I was desperate to watch Top of the Pops but, bad timing BBC, I was being a good girl at the meeting at 7 o'clock every Thursday night.

From somewhere deep inside a silly, uninvited thought entered my head. I suddenly felt as though something was going to happen to stop me from entering this den of worldliness. Did I need to be saved from myself? Maybe at the last minute a huge eagle would sweep down and pick me up in its scratchy talons. It would carry me, feet dangling, white shoes sparkling, all the way across town, over the rooftops, the railway line and the marshy fields and gently place me on the ground outside the doors of the Kingdom Hall. I would be safe there. Back in the fold with no harm done. What a lucky escape!

I shook the stupid thought from my mind. No. This was my choice. My choice to indulge in an activity so alien to other Witnesses and highly discouraged. This would be an act that would have me hauled before the Elders in the back room of the

Kingdom Hall, I would be given a serious talking to and, if I made going to nightclubs a habit, I would see my friends start to distance themselves from me and mark me as 'bad association.' But I'm not living under those rules any longer. No. I am exercising my right to weigh up the options and make wise choices with all I've learned throughout my life, and I would make tonight a successful and enjoyable night despite the torrent of conflicting emotions bombarding me. I walked through those flashing doors with my head held high, wondering what exciting things the night was going to bring.

But my determination was short-lived as once again, I found myself hiding in the ladies' toilet. Hands behind my back, I leaned against the cool tiled wall. It seemed the ladies were becoming my go-to place in times of great stress. The music was so loud out there and all I could hear once inside the quiet of the toilets was the ringing in my ears. I wasn't dealing with this nightclub experience very well. My conscience was working overtime and the things I saw, that I had never witnessed before, made me want to get as far from that place as I could. I had to get some perspective.

I stood in front of the large rectangular mirror above the row of pink sinks. It was quite filthy in there. In the top right-hand corner of the mirror, squiggles of purple lipstick announced that, "Spinney sucks!" *What does that mean*? I wondered. I had no idea. Perhaps Spinney had a set of false teeth which he'd lost while swimming in the sea and now he was reduced to sucking? Poor Spinney. A streamer of toilet roll, decorated with dusty footprints, ran from one cubicle out to the entrance door and a dried-up mascara wand floated in a blocked sink half-full of grey water. Wads of hair picked out from grooming utensils had been left all over the tops and a dainty tampon (unused thankfully) sat alone in the corner on the floor. A girl rushed into an empty cubicle and didn't even bother to close the door before her knickers were down, a sigh of relief escaping from her lips as she plonked herself down on the seat. Girls shouting, squealing, some crying, some laughing, blowing their noses, reapplying make-up. There was more activity in those toilets than I'd seen in any others, ever.

Despite my bird's nest hair my reflected face reminded me of my mum. Oh God! Mum! What am I doing here?! She would do her nut if she knew what sort of establishment I was in right now. She'd tell me to run! Run for your life!!

I placed my hands on my hips, leaned in close to the graffitied mirror and told myself in no uncertain terms: *Pull yourself together girl, it's music and dancing, something you've wanted to do for years. So what if that couple on the sofa are snogging the faces off each other, let them get on with it. What if that girl's skirt comes to just below her knickers, look the other way if it offends you. DJ Spinney is playing some really good music, just concentrate on that and ignore everything else. Will is here, he'll protect you. Nothing bad will happen as long as you stay close to him. In fact, if this place was really the Devil's Den surely Will wouldn't have brought you here. Chill out, relax. Have another drink and then get back out there on that dance floor. This is your new life, the one you've chosen. You're nineteen years old, and it's time you got used to living in the real world.*

My shoes were killing me. I wasn't sure how much longer I could keep them on my feet let alone walk or dance in them. Behind me I heard toilet roll being torn off and scrunched up. I was boiling hot, the sweat running down my back making me feel itchy. I pushed up the sleeves of my glittery batwing top and tried to pull the hem of my pleather skirt down below my knees. It hadn't felt too immodest in the shop but now that I was actually in the correct environment for such an outfit, I was very conscious of it. If my knees were showing some bloke would surely think I'm asking for it. I resolved to get into the middle of the crowd of friends I was with and stay there.

Sandy and Ellie must have followed me in and, after both flushing their toilets at the same time, immerged from the cubicles reaching for the bars of soap.

"Always wash your hands at this place, Jess. You never know what you might pick up." Sandy wiped her hands on the roll of towelling issued from the clunking dispenser and, hand in hand, the two girls headed for the door. Ellie held out her hand out behind her for me to grab which I was grateful for in that moment. We trotted out in our high heels, Sandy in her DMs, and after eventually being served at the bar, went back out on the sticky dancefloor. I tried very hard to manoeuvre myself around to the area in front of DJ Spinney. I wanted to see if he actually had any teeth but he kept his head down in concentration all the time. I kept a smile on my face while I danced and no one would have guessed the depth of my fears.

I don't remember how I got home. Will told me we got a taxi in the early hours. Esther had waited up for us and, as she always did when Will had been out with his friends, had made us bacon and egg rolls to soak up some of the alcohol we'd consumed. I don't know what she must have thought of me. I hope I didn't say anything I shouldn't have. Apparently, I wolfed down my food and a pint of water before I eventually went up to bed, muttering and singing some unrecognisable tune. I don't recall any of it.

"Ugh," was the only sound I could muster the next morning. The pain in my head was indescribable as I tried to raise myself up in the bed. But it was no use. I wasn't going anywhere. "Ugh," came out again as I held my head between my palms. I could barely open my eyes.

Light spilled through the door as it opened and someone padded across the carpet towards me.

"Oh, poor you! Rough night, was it?" It was Will, and I heard him chuckling as he placed a mug on the bedside table.

"Water! I need water, quick!" I moaned.

"It's hot, strong, sweet coffee you need after the amount you drank last night, Jess."

"Stop shouting, it hurts."

"Come on you, let's get you up," he instructed, which was the last thing I wanted to do. My stomach was churning and I don't think I've ever felt so ill before or since. I managed to get myself down the stairs and into the kitchen. Thank goodness for banisters. Will announced that Esther had gone out and that he was going for a swim. His head was all right. He was used to these nights out, unlike me.

"I'll take Petra with me, she's been itching to go out. Walkies Petra! There are some eggs left in the fridge if you feel like eating." I so wished he would stop shouting.

He kissed me on the cheek and ruffled my already untidy hair and, after looking at me sideways and giggling again, he left with Petra scampering after him. I sat slumped in my dressing gown at the kitchen table, my hand around my mug of coffee. My clutch bag stared up at me having spilled its contents across the surface where I must have chucked it down last night. The crumpled entrance ticket to Dixieland, my burgundy lipstick, and an artificial red rose, it's wire stem bent in several places. Where did that come from? No idea.

How much did I actually drink? I was only on lager shandies and they'd never made me feel this bad before. OK, I had never drunk more than a couple at once and I know I had more than that but surely it's not strong enough to make me unable to remember getting home. It must have been a combination of the loud music, the heavy atmosphere, perhaps the lack of clean air to breathe given the thickness of the smoke, that made my brain block out half the night's events. Yes, that was it.

Suddenly the churning in my stomach stepped up a notch and I instinctually wrapped my arms around my middle. Forget the coffee, a pint of water will settle it down, I thought, as I made my way across to the sink. Glugging back the cool liquid and steadying myself on the counter the sudden sound of the doorbell made me jump. It was a very loud ring, such as is necessary in a large house. The unwelcome noise set my head pulsating again and with the cool glass against my forehead I trod carefully across the hall to open the front door. I couldn't believe my eyes.

"Good morning!" This voice was far too chirpy. "We're making brief calls in this area, hoping to share with you an encouraging thought from the Bible."

This was the last thing I needed right now. While they waited for my response I couldn't help but notice, even through blurred vision, that the two young men standing there looked so smart. Very well presented, their hair neatly combed, shoes polished to a high shine and each wore a friendly smile, 'the Kingdom smile,' it was called. Overly sincere, thus making it false in my humble opinion. I'd flashed that smile so often myself in the past, I should know.

Shame I wiped it off their faces so quickly. I didn't mean to, really, it just came up out of nowhere. I couldn't utter a single word as I felt the greasy, gaseous mass of last night's bacon and egg roll rising up inside me. A sharp pain in my belly accompanied by a sudden lurch and out shot a watery torrent the colour of a muddy puddle and the texture of Branston pickle, landing all over the younger one's tailored jacket. He took an involuntary step back but it wasn't quick enough. With arms outstretched he looked down in dismay at the state of him and back up at me, a grimace spreading across his freshly shaved face.

"Ugh!" I muttered as I covered my mouth. I didn't know what to do or even what to say. I frantically looked around for any kind of clue and grabbed the box of tissues from the telephone table and threw it at him. I muttered some "sorry"s and slammed the door shut. With the help of the banister I stumbled up the stairs, fell into bed face down and pulled the covers over my head.

"But I don't understand how I could possibly feel so ill when I'd only had a few shandies, Will." Later that day Will informed me that yes, I'd had about six shandies but I'd also had four whiskies as well. Then more shandies. Oh. That'll be it then.

"Lesson learned?"

"Mmm, maybe. It was a really good night, wasn't it?" Thankfully, all I could remember was the fun of being with good people and the music that made me feel happy and alive.

"Sandy and Ellie were just hilarious," I reminded Will and we laughed at the overly expressive dance they'd done to Bananarama's 'Love in the First Degree'. A small audience had surrounded them as they moved in ways only drunk people could. It was like a dancing conversation with Sandy questioning and Ellie answering and both miming the narrative, holding imaginary mics. I'd never seen anything like it.

"Not as funny as the greeting you gave those two at the front door, I hear!"

I'd told Will about the episode but found it completely embarrassing. I hoped he would remain as discreet as he'd been so far and wouldn't tell everyone how badly I handled my alcohol. Time to change the subject.

"Er, how was your swim this morning, Will?"

Living right on the beach at Pevensey Bay was such a special thing. The sand and pebbles stretched for miles each way, interwoven with golden samphire and sea holly. The imperfection of the worn and broken groynes did not detract from the beauty of the area but instead gave evidence of its history, mechanised shingle-shoving being necessary on many occasions over the years.

The impenetrable Martello Tower at Langney Point was faintly visible to the west, and Hastings and Bexhill swept off to the east. In front, the vast sea whose colour changed with the sky. It called to me each morning, cold as it was, but several months of morning swims had built up my tolerance for the temperature. In the depths of winter, when it really was too cold, I swam at the Leisure Pool, a fifteen-minute walk along the beach towards Eastbourne. I'm sure it helped my mental health. Helped me to see things clearer, made me feel cleansed each time I emerged, as if I could simply let all the hurt of the past run off me into the ground, to be washed away forever.

Esther had been so kind to invite me to live here. She was non-judgemental, considerate and just let me be who I wanted to be. But I didn't want to disappoint her, though, so I kept her involved in a lot of my decisions and frequently asked for her advice. Between the support of both Esther and Will I had found myself in almost full-time employment back at the Beefeater, I'd met some lovely people, I had a gym and swimming membership and – something I'd never dreamed I would ever have – a social life!

Will came over from his home in Brighton most weekends and we hit the town on a Friday and or Saturday night. Cinema, restaurant, pub quiz, a meal at home with Will's family joining us. It all seemed very normal. I'd been told that anyone that wasn't a Jehovah's Witness was a 'worldly' person, full of deceit and lies. They were habitual adulterers, thieves, corrupt and not to be trusted. By turning away the Witnesses at their door they had rejected God himself and therefore would not be spared at Armageddon. They were as good as dead.

Such a message, when drummed into a child's mind, becomes the only truth they know. But this was a different reality. I could see for myself that these people were not like that. They had qualities I hadn't even seen in so-called Christians in the congregation. Unlike the Witnesses they didn't keep a written record of how much time they spent encouraging someone, how much effort they had put in to helping a local charity or how much money they had donated to a worthy cause. It was done from the heart and no trumpets were needed to announce their good deeds.

It was so refreshing.

As I often did on a bright day I sat on the low wall at the front of the house when the sun was at its highest. The seagulls were bothering the beach-goers, life was ticking along nicely and all felt right with the world. For the first time in many months I felt at peace. I missed my mum, of course, and had been back up to see her a couple of times. Our regular phone conversations were a little stilted and usually short, but she was ok. I think she may have even been a little bit happy for me. I had worried that she may have descended into another deep depressive state again after I'd left, but she didn't. She became more active in the ministry and was getting a regular lift to the meetings instead of having to take two buses. Those things helped her enormously, I know.

My brother Peter had been in touch with mum's doctor, too, to help her with finding the correct amount of medication, anti-depressants. As far as I could see, and as far as mum allowed me to know, she was going fine. It probably helped having her teenage daughter out of the way. Her trust in me had disappeared after I got disfellowshipped and she must have feared that I would end up in the same position again. It was always stressful for the whole family when someone gets disfellowshipped. I'd seen it in other families. Being instructed to shun them, not interact with them on any level must be a huge pressure. And the fear of being caught talking to that person and then being disfellowshipped themselves will be on everyone's mind too. So, the fact that I had moved away from mum probably meant she could relax a lot more. And Jehovah's Witnesses say they do not split up families!

Will joined me on the wall and we watched the beach activity for precisely seven minutes. Wordlessly we rose and walked hand in hand along the pebbly beach towards the Aqua Bar. We went there often, and I began to notice some regulars.

Nods of acknowledgement became the norm as we entered and walked towards our favourite table by the window. On one occasion a couple walked in holding hands who I thought I recognised. They did a double take when they saw me and then nodded. I was still trying to work out where I knew them from so there wasn't time to give them a nod back before they'd sat down.

Will ordered at the bar, a light lunch, then we would cook in the evening. He was a good cook, like his mum, and we'd been experimenting with different recipes over the months to get some variety into our diet. But I begged him to give up trying to get me to eat seafood. Cod and chips I'd stretch to but nothing with legs, eyes or a tail, please.

They kept looking over at us.

"Do you know them?" Will whispered without looking their way. "They certainly know you."

"I vaguely recognise them." I racked my brain to think where I'd seen them before and then it dawned on me. Of course, the Kingdom Hall. Eastbourne Congregation. They were one of those couples that were into everybody's business. If you wanted to know anything, just ask the Peacocks, Ginny and Geoff, they'll tell you.

Lunch finished, Will stood up to go. He had a work appointment. His work as a freelance photographer kept him busy and he had the option to turn down weekend appointments if he so wished. But this job was worth the money so with apologies for not being able to spend as much time together this weekend, he kissed my cheek across the table and squeezed my hand and grabbed his jacket.

"I don't know how long this is going to take so I'll see you later this evening."

"Take your time, I'm going over to Sandy and Ellie's after this so, yeah, see you later. Have fun." We exchanged more kisses, blown over our empty plates, and he was gone. I really didn't mind a bit of time on my own. It gave me the chance to think, to plan, to absorb and process my new life.

It took just five minutes to scrunch back to the house, trying to stay on the smaller pebbles and not run the risk of breaking my ankle on the bigger uneven rocks. As I approached the side door I heard a faint voice off to my right. A weak, "Jessica!" tumbled out of Ginny Peacock's mouth which I almost didn't hear.

"Sorry, we're not following you, ha, ha, the car's parked just down here. How are you these days? How's your mum? Is this where you live now, then?" She asked so many questions. My family, well most of it till we all split up, went to the meetings in Eastbourne for several years. I recalled Geoff partnering Peter on the ministry several times on a Saturday morning but we couldn't really call them our friends.

"I'm very well thanks, Ginny. I couldn't quite place you at first, sorry about that."

I didn't have to answer anyone's questions. My life was now none of their business. Neither should it have been but they made it their business by describing the organisation as 'one big happy family'. Everyone seemed to be in each others' pockets which opened the door to judgement, back-biting, nosiness, passing on stories without checking if they were even true and Chinese whispers. I wanted no more of that. After all, the scripture actually said at 1 Thessalonians 4:11 to "...mind your own business..." I decided to turn the conversation around.

"Lovely day today, feels like spring is finally here." I unlocked the door and made to hold Petra back as she bounded out to greet me. "Sorry, got to go. Get in Petra! Come on girl. Bye," I waved, "nice to see you."

A couple of weak "bye"s reached me across the patio and they shuffled off, looking back and up at the house.

I didn't want to get into conversation with any Jehovah's Witnesses. Not on any level. That section of my life was over. I had no desire to revisit any part of it. Deep inside I was still recovering from the Elder's, or should I say, the Presiding Overseer of the congregation Kevin Choi's, decision to disfellowship me after I'd made a mistake. A mistake that most teenagers make – I'd ended up having sex with a boy I wasn't married to. But I was assured they were simply sticking to scriptural instruction: I had not shown enough genuine repentance because I hadn't immediately fled the scene of the crime. No matter that I was in a tent in the middle of Norfolk with no money. So, the judiciary meeting following my confession, which consisted of myself facing three elders and no support from my mum or anyone else, ended with their decision to disfellowship me. It had shocked me. I'd hoped to get away with a telling off, my guilt was enough to weigh me down and I was on the floor already, but no. They clearly thought I needed to be taught a lesson. The announcement was made to the congregation about a week later and from that moment the silence descended.

But who was I to argue with the Elders? They were assigned by God himself to care for the spiritual needs of the congregation, so to get rid of me, an evil fornicator, in order to protect the rest of the congregation was only right. My reinstatement after more than a year of isolation and depression had left me with many unanswered questions and such anger about how the Elders had the right to treat people in that way. I knew that Kevin Choi's answers to those questions, though, would never have satisfied me. There was nothing he could have possibly said to make me feel better about their harsh treatment.

No. Words, simply would not do.

I didn't consciously plan to do it. I'd just got so angry after hearing a very judgmental talk given one Sunday meeting by Kevin himself. That was the last straw for me. His descriptive words were about the wicked people of this world being snuffed out at Armageddon like a flame, puff! Gone! The audience had laughed and applauded and their reaction disgusted me. I realised in that moment he was talking about anyone who had rejected the Witnesses at their door, and that included my dad, my sisters, my school mates, teachers, Esther, Will.

It was the most evil thing I'd ever heard.

When the meeting had finished I approached Kevin in the foyer, my anger boiled over and expressed itself with my right knee meeting his groin with all the force I could muster. I followed up with my hand forming a tight fist. It crunched against the gristle in his nose as I took a swing and sent him flying backwards through the glass doors to the gasps of the audience.

My god, it felt good.

CHAPTER 3

I wondered if word of that wonderfully satisfying event had reached Eastbourne congregation. News always seemed to spread exceptionally fast amongst the Witnesses. But it was never classed as 'gossip.' No, it was "concern for our Brothers and Sisters in these trying times." Bollocks.

I recognised that my language had become filthy since I'd struck out on my own, since I was no longer living in that cocoon of spongy protection surrounded by meek and mild weasels. I was trying to explain to Will one day just how I would feel if I ever bumped into Kevin Choi again, perhaps when I was up in the Midlands visiting mum. I said that under no circumstances would I engage in conversation with him and that if he persisted in trying to preach to me I would politely tell him to fuck the fucking hell away from me and to never fucking well attempt to bloody fucking talk to me again.

Will laughed.

"I'm serious! Why are you laughing? That man is responsible for Alan taking his own life. He also made me think about doing the same!"

Will just kept laughing. I didn't understand. Tears were starting to well up because I thought he wasn't taking me seriously. He'd always been so understanding, so why start to mock me now?

"Jessica, come here. Sit down," he invited me, as he pulled out a chair from the table. I sat down miserably in front of him as he'd asked. As he took my face in his hands and looked me directly in the eyes his softness overwhelmed me and I just wanted to hold him.

"Jess, you need to learn how to swear properly. Right, we're going to try a little experiment, so just do as I ask." I wondered what on earth he had in mind. "Tell me to fuck off."

"Fuck off," I mumbled, moving my head down. I didn't want to play this silly game.

"No, come on. Really, tell me to fuck off."

"Fuck off," I said to his face, and shook his hands off mine.

"Fuck, off, fuck off, fuck off!!" He was beginning to annoy me now.

I rose to my feet and pushed him in the chest. "Fuck off, fuck off, fuck off!!" I shouted as he stumbled back. The look of shock on his face took me by surprise. Petra barked and started circling the two of us in confusion. After a moment's silence a smirk broke out on my face, I couldn't help it, and then we both ended up laughing long and hard. Petra settled down again but kept a worried look on her face. My subsequent lesson in cussing consisted of sounding out many other swear words and discussing how to use them (some completely new to me) and it felt kind of liberating to shout and curse at the top of my voice. I used them freely for a while, only amongst others around me that did the same, never in front of Esther, noticing others' reactions to my new, grown-up, fruity language skills. But almost everyone told me: "it doesn't suit you, Jess, it just sounds funny when you use that filthy language." So in the end I stopped. I'd have to find alternative words to express my anger.

That evening I spent with Sandy and Ellie at their place and it proved to be a revelatory event. I'd been there before, some months previously, when they'd had a few friends round for drinks but this was the first time they'd invited just me. This was my chance to get to know them a bit better, find out what made them tick. They were so much fun to be with, so carefree and laid back. Sandy had a bit of a fiery temper as I'd witnessed when Ellie lost the front door keys. Her language had been choice and loud but Ellie just took it on the chin and told her to stop being such an arse. The keys were hiding in the bottom of her bag and she dangled them in front of Sandy's face with glee on their retrieval.

Sandy said she worked in an office. 'In an office' could mean she did one of a hundred different jobs. I pushed myself to pry a bit and it turned out she'd been working for an insurance company for a few years. Started off as a filing clerk, then an audio typist and more recently she had been put forward for some training in the business. Exams were offered and qualifications – bits of paper that said she was intelligent, as I joked with her. Ellie was sticking it out at college doing a hairdressing course. She hated it. She said she'd rather wear the hair instead of creating the hair on someone else's head. But it will get her a qualification and that's what she needed. It would free her up to work anywhere in the country. They were both stable in their jobs and knew where they were going.

But there we go again with stuff I didn't know anything about. I needed to find out, properly, how to go about my life. How to get somewhere. How to move forward and start planning my future. Pioneer? No thank you. I wanted to use my God-given brain, exercise my thinking faculties, learn a new subject that I might just be able to make a living from. I loved living at Esther's house. It was perfect for me, spacious with good bus routes and within walking distance to shops and leisure. But the reality was, I couldn't stay there forever. I needed to know what to do in order to one day have my own place.

How much money would I need to live independently? For instance, how much does a flat like this cost to rent? What about paying the bills, and food? Sandy runs a car so she much be on a decent wage. I decided to take the bull by the horns and ask some specific questions and hope the girls didn't think I was being too personal about their finances.

Ellie had finished pottering around in the kitchen after our takeaway of fish and chips had been cleared up. Time for a nice cool lager now to cut through all that grease. I'd brought along two packs of four cans and Ellie peeled the first three out of the plastic holder and handed one each to Sandy and me. She fell heavily onto the sofa beside Sandy and leant her head against her shoulder. Sandy readjusted herself and threaded an arm around Ellie's back. They were so close, just like I imagined sisters would be. I thought about my own sisters who had left early on in my life and felt a momentary pang of something with such strength behind it. Loss? Grief? As if I had mislaid something important and couldn't find it. I wasn't able to name it but it was painful. I put my feet up on the footstool and, leaning my head back, I sighed into the room, a sigh of total relaxation, in a peaceful, warm environment. I thought it was time to start digging.

"So, what's this then, a two bedroom flat? I hope you don't mind me asking but what would this set me back in the way of rent, Sandy? Do you get any of your bills included?"

My enquiry was simple and I'd hope she would help me by getting out a pen and some paper to write some figures down. I was not expecting her answer to be what it was. And it completely threw me. I had no idea. My naivety had caught me out again and made me feel like a complete idiot.

The flat had just the one bedroom.

The girls been an item for three years, having met at Dixieland, of all places. When I realised the nature of their relationship I nearly spluttered my lager but managed to turn it into a discreet cough. I think they knew I hadn't figured it out up to now. Looking back, the signs were all there, the secret glances, displays of affection, a sneaky kiss – just the same as any couple in love. They didn't try to hide anything, I just wasn't that observant.

But this put a different spin on things. My upbringing had taught me that homosexuality and lesbianism was wrong. Plain and simple. It had no place in Christianity, was abhorrent to God and

Christ. The numerous examples in the Bible of such goings on had all ended in the gay ones being destroyed. Warnings about what would happen to such sinners at Armageddon were clear to read and there was never any doubt in my mind that this kind of behaviour was not to be condoned in any way. I had to make a choice.

But Sandy and Ellie were my friends. What do I do now? I felt immediate sadness at the realisation that I would have to cease mixing with them. If I continued I would no doubt become like them, and their sinful influence would lead me to sink to their level, perhaps even taking up the practice myself. All this had been drummed into me from such an early age and was never questioned or analysed, by anyone. It was just accepted that, as the scripture says: 'Bad associations spoil useful habits.' It only took a few seconds to spring to mind in a flash and the curtain came down. It was simple, there was no decision to make, what was I thinking? My friendship with those girls, or whatever they wanted to call themselves, was well and truly over.

I steered the conversation round to an appropriate completion and started to make my excuses.

"Got an early swim before work tomorrow so I need to get back," I announced firmly.

"But it's not even 8 o'clock yet, stay and have another can. Sandy'll run you home," Ellie pleaded.

"Nah, but thanks anyway. Best get off."

They looked at each other, then back at me, and I saw a frown form on Ellie's forehead. Neither of them said any more as I left the flat and made my way back home. I truly didn't want to offend them, they'd been so good to me, but I felt them clock my tension and the damage had been done. I left their flat, their little love nest, their shag-pad and walked the four miles back home feeling oh, so self-righteous and pleased with myself that I'd stood up for my beliefs. And I'd done it all on my own, with no one behind me quoting scriptures, nobody standing in the wings ready to pounce and judge me should I have got it wrong. For a short while it felt good.

Will arrived home as I was making a cup of tea. It felt so natural for him to walk up behind me and put his arms around my waist. I left the tea leaves to brew in the pot and turned to face him, my arms wrapped around his back.

"Did you know about Sandy and Ellie?" I had to ask.

"Know what?" He looked stumped as he peered down at me. I couldn't say the 'L' word. It was too abhorrent.

"You know. Their relationship."

"Oh, yeah, they've been together for ages. It never entered my head to say anything, they're just Sandy and Ellie." I could see a cloud descend over him as he suddenly realised that this was a big thing for me to take in.

"Perhaps I should have told you, but I thought you'd figured it out."

"I can't see them anymore, Will." I shook my head. It's just so wrong. They're great and I really like them, both of them, but there's no grey area in the Bible for this one."

He huffed. "I thought you were leaving all that behind you, you know, not being told what to think and do and feel anymore. Making your own decisions."

"I am but I still want to be a Christian, I *think*, I'm not sure. But anyway, Christ's direct instruction is that those who practice homosexuality will be destroyed at Armageddon. It's clear as day."

"And you still believe Armageddon's coming, do you?"

Another thing to think about. I huffed at him.

"Of course I do! I mean, I think so. The world is in a terrible state and the Governments are not solving anything, in fact things are getting worse as time goes on. And God's the only one that can sort things out properly, for good." I tutted at myself as those familiar words spewed out. I didn't want to sound like I was on someone's doorstep, preaching to them.

"And you still believe in God, do you? And Jesus Christ? And that there are angels flying around in Heaven. Do you believe in Heaven?" Will was starting to annoy me by throwing all these questions at me, like a barrage of bullets, one after the other with no time to form a thought, let alone a reasonable answer. Up to now I was so sure that the teachings of Christ were the model to live by, that his ways were the best in order to live peacefully with others and have a happy life. The reality was that I'd only ever heard the JW interpretation of his words. Could I be sure they had been telling me it correctly? And beyond that, Will was absolutely right to ask me: do I actually believe in God?

These were huge issues and the sudden and unexpected doubt thrown up by these questions blew my mind. I felt as though I'd been punched in the stomach as the realisation dawned on me: what if none of it was true? What if I'd been lied to all my life? Perhaps there is no god, it's just been a means to control society, an Association with its own set of rules. Where would that leave me? I put my head in my hands and closed my eyes. Will guided me to a chair at the kitchen table.

"I'm sorry, Jess. I don't mean to attack your faith and your beliefs." He sighed heavily and pulled my hands down, covering them with his.

"Perhaps you need to do a bit of investigating. Find out what other people believe. The way I see it, for the last nineteen years you've been taught a certain set of beliefs and it's going to take quite a while to unlearn these things and then find out what you believe for yourself. You're going to have to be patient."

What he said made sense.

"How did you get to be so wise, Will?" He smiled with his eyes, as he often did, and in that moment I wished I could have just melted into his arms, forget about what's right and wrong and who decides which is which and just rest my brain for a while. But, in order for me to be free enough to move forward, I needed my own answers to these serious questions.

So, investigate? Where on earth would I start? What point would there be in examining another set of beliefs, different to my long-held ones? After all, they would only be another person's interpretation of the same book, the Bible, and that wouldn't get me anywhere. To study each religion in turn would take a lifetime and sounded like such hard work.

Perhaps I should just talk to people in general, individuals, and get a feel for what they hold to be true, what they cling on to, to help them get through the day. What do they think is happening to the planet? What happens when we die? Do the good go to heaven, the wicked to hell? Is there a purgatory, a holding room until God decides our ultimate fate? Why is there so much illness, starvation, poverty, crime, corruption, shootings; does man bring it on himself? Is the devil to blame? Is behaviour inherited?

Why do families break up? Why do marriages break down? Why are there so many children growing up with only one parent? Why did my dad leave? Why do people take drugs? Why do some get drunk on a daily basis? Why did my sisters leave? Mental illness, what causes it and is there a proper cure, a permanent cure? Why is my mum like she is? So cold, aloof and unapproachable, unaffectionate? Why, why, why?

There was just too much to contemplate. My thoughts gave me a banging headache.

Sundays were the best day of the week. No meeting to go to for a start. Even though I hadn't been attending for over a year that was the first thought on waking up every Sunday morning, stretching into the daylight: 'no meeting today!' Beach followed by breakfast. Will usually stayed over on a Saturday night and we could eat on the patio now that the June sunshine was warm from early in the day. Petra felt the heat with her thick coat and found some shade under the swing seat. She didn't seem to mind being nudged with a foot as we gently swung to and fro.

Activity on the beach, human and canine, increased with the temperature and the dots of colour spreading east and west moved up the shore as the tide made its way in. A sandcastle was slowly destroyed as the waves lapped its edges, the moat filling and emptying with the flow of the frothy water.

"Fancy dinner at The Castle later on? Give mum a break from cooking a Sunday roast?"

"Sounds good, yeah."

The Castle Inn was the best pub in the village and served great food, hot and plenty of it. The food at the Beefeater was good pub grub but The Castle's creations seemed to be presented with a little more care. We spent the day pottering around, tidying, sorting letters and junk mail delivered during the week. I took a bucket of hot water out the front to see if I could scrub away the rings left by the milk bottles, brushed around the step and shook out the doormat.

I didn't need to dress up just to go to the pub but I did put a bit of makeup on. Esther always looked her best, always dressed well, considerately, well-coordinated and I thought, *I hope I scrub up as well as her when I'm her age.*

The roast beef went down well; the three of us had the same. Stomachs full we moved from the dining table and relaxed into three tub chairs positioned in front of the fire, fresh flowers in the hearth, and ordered a big pot of tea.

Over in the corner sat a man who caught my eye. He was quite alone. Dressed in shabby trousers, the hem falling down on one of them, his hair unkempt and two, maybe three days' worth of stubble on his chin. I wondered if he smelled, and that's why he's alone. He'd finished eating and sat reading the paper in silence, looking as if he would rather not be disturbed. He shook the journal as he turned another page, eyes starting at the top left-hand side.

"You know who that is, don't you?" Esther remarked.

"No, should I?" I asked, curious, wondering if he was once famous or rich and had now fallen on hard times.

"That's Scissors."

Scissors was a local character known by everyone. He'd been in and around Pevensey Bay for many years. A sharpener of knives, a fixer of lawn mowers, he was the person people turned to if they needed anything practical doing that they couldn't do themselves. He was very helpful and was willing to be paid in cash or beer, vegetables from gardens, apples or wood for his fire. If you needed a job doing, Scissors was your man. He had no phone but could usually be found around the village or in his corner down the pub. He was even known for cutting hair. But really he should have been called 'Shears' as that was what he used for those haircuts. No shaping, just cutting and all the same style. Esther had sent Will to him; once, and only once. He came back crying saying he couldn't go back to school with his hair like that, no, not even with a hat on.

"The haircuts were bad enough," Esther recounted, "but the story of the Christmas turkey took the biscuit."

Will laughed out loud, Esther nudged and shushed him.

The story went that a local man had forgotten to order his turkey from the butcher one Christmas, years ago, and went to Scissors for help.

Esther took up the story: ""You gotta help me, Scissors. I've told the wife I'm picking up the bird tomorrow morning but I didn't actually order one. Butcher's got none left. Don't know what I'm gonna do," he said. Stop snorting, Will. Anyway, Scissors calmed him down and said, "leave it to me I'll sort you out, mate." So, Scissors asked around at other places about any spare turkeys for sale but there were none."

She shuffled on her seat, glancing over to the man in the corner and continued, almost conspiratorially.

"So, the next morning he turned up at this man's house with a huge bag and presented him with his Christmas dinner, one or two stray feathers floating about. "My god, you're a life-saver, mate. I can't thank you enough," he said. Problem solved. A few days later he sees Scissors in the street and runs over to shake his hand. "Ah, Scissors, that was the best Christmas turkey I've ever had, mate. And it was huge! I've never tasted anything like it. As I said, you're a life-saver. Where on earth did you get it from so late in the day?"

Will and Esther looked at each other and Esther revealed that on Christmas eve at midnight Scissors had sneaked into Princes Park risking a hefty fine and a stretch at Her Majesty's pleasure for stealing one of her swans.

When the penny dropped my hand shot up to my mouth as I felt something between disgust, amusement and horror at such a thing.

"There was no problem too tough for Scissors but when the locals found out they gave him a wide berth after that," Esther explained. "That's why he's always on his own now probably – he crossed a line."

The pub doors swung open as our laughter ebbed away and I took a long swig of my lager, peering over the rim of the glass. In walked a couple of familiar faces through the double swing doors. I groaned inwardly. It was them again – the Peacocks. I took that moment to visit the ladies, for a genuine reason this time, not to calm my nerves. As I emerged, I hoped they hadn't noticed me but sadly they had chosen the table right next to ours, making it impossible to avoid them.

"Hi, Jess," came a cheery greeting from Ginny as she leant across the table and waved.

"Hi, Ginny." I didn't want to get into a conversation and was eager to leave.

"Shall we head home? There's ice cream in the freezer, we could have that instead of ordering a sweet," I suggested. I didn't give Will and Esther much choice as I speedily slipped into my jacket and started moving towards the exit.

"Making a hasty retreat. What's that all about then?" Will enquired when we got outside.

"Just don't want to be around those people, they make me cringe with their sickly sweetness all the time. Don't want to be anywhere near them," I explained.

"You've got to get over it, girl." Esther was right, I would have to overcome the feelings they produced in me. I would have to, one day, risk having a friendly chat and be prepared for them to twist it round to the Truth, which was an inevitable part of any conversation with a Witness. I'd have to learn how to hold my own with them.

But not today.

Our walk home was fast-paced and direct, personally I was eager to get that ice cream down my neck. Esther put her feet up in the lounge and I made her a cup of tea. She got her head into the newspaper and seemed to be in her own little world. She was a very hard worker, on her feet most of the time at the hospital and she actually deserved a break. I wondered how long it had been since she'd had a holiday. Certainly not since I'd been living here. I would suggest it to her sometime.

Will was messing around with Petra while I tidied the worktops in the kitchen and put things back in the cupboards. The bin needed emptying and the milk bottles putting outside the front door. I was proud that I could carry four bottles in one hand and made my way to the door. It was just starting to get a bit cooler and as I stood on the step the slither of a new moon caught my eye. I breathed in the cool air and shocked myself by saying a quick prayer to give thanks for the beauty of God's creation. I looked around to see if anyone had heard me even though I'd said it in my mind. Silly!

Something else caught my eye just up the road. A car I thought I recognised. Just as the thought entered my head the owners turned the corner and came into view, walking boldly towards me.

"Jessica, twice in one day. How funny."

Not funny, really, as you've parked right outside my house. I considered as my reply.

"Ginny, Geoff. Nice meal at the Castle, then?"

"Oh, no we just had a small glass of wine each. Geoff likes to cook on a Sunday after the meeting."

"I thought you lived in the village now. What's with the car?"

"Erm, we……we'd been for a drive earlier so parked here on the way back instead of going home and coming back out again." Geoff didn't often speak, just stood by Ginny's side and nodded in the right places. But he was very quick to jump in with his explanation.

"Is this your boyfriend's car, then? Nice," he said, leaning back and admiring the chrome on the car behind. I had a Golf back in the day."

I didn't confirm or deny that it was Will's car. It was none of their business. They struck me as such a weird couple – nosey and intrusive but beyond that I thought no more of the conversation.

CHAPTER 4

It was June, and Margaret Thatcher had been re-elected as Prime Minister for a third term. The BBC news was on the TV as I joined Esther in the sun lounge. "Thatcher's parliamentary majority was reduced to 102 compared to the 144-seat majority gained at the election four years earlier," so the newscaster declared.

"Hello, darling. Just a minute, I just want to hear this news about the election. I was going to stay up last night for the results but after the day I'd had at work I couldn't keep my eyes open."

I sat in silence as the programme continued. Esther looked dismayed for some reason. Political language was something I'd never needed to learn so whatever was coming out of the reporter's mouth was a complete mystery to me. Ballot? Conceded? Landslide?

Jehovah's Witnesses were not to get involved with politics, neither on a local or national level. In fact, it was a disfellowshipping offence. Yes, if you were found to be voting on a regular basis then you clearly show that you do not put your trust in God to sort out the world's problems. There was no place for you in the congregation. Out you go. I remember in secondary school I was put forward for the school council as one of the teachers had noticed I brought up points that no one else did. But mum persuaded me it would not be a good idea. No, being involved in making decisions affecting pupils would mean spending more time, probably after school, with worldly teenagers. And no-one really knows all the ins and outs of a matter, so to be involved in making decisions without full knowledge of a subject would lead to disappointment and regret. You may wish to do good and be sincere in what you plan to do if you were voted in but rarely would you be able to fulfil your promises. It would just result in letting your supporters down. They would be upset, you would be upset and nothing would improve. You're best staying out of it.

It was simple in the Truth. A very black or white world. There was an answer to every dilemma, every problem, within the pages of the Watchtower and Awake magazines produce by the Society. No one needed to think for themselves, ever.

"Well, let's see what she'll be changing this time. Yet more cuts to the health service no doubt, and the Poll Tax will come into force." Esther sighed as she rose from her chair and moved towards the kitchen. "Time for a brew," she called.

"Esther, do you vote? I'm guessing you voted Labour." I followed behind.

"You're right. Always voted Labour, as did my parents before me. You have that privilege now you're over eighteen. Have you given it much thought?"

"Ha! I wouldn't know where to start!"

"It's a minefield, politics, I'll give you that. Highs and lows, expectations and disappointments.

Doesn't matter which party you vote for, they're all the same on that score. I guess the important thing is exercising your right to use your vote. You must have learned about the Suffragettes at school?"

A fascinating lesson followed about the efforts of the women of the Suffragette movement and how they campaigned fiercely to get women the vote. It was an eye opener to me, I'd never heard of them before.

"So, you see, Jess, it's important to not waste your vote, otherwise the efforts of those women would be in vain. All their suffering, their hunger strikes, arrests, being manhandled by men, which would have been shocking to the women back then, as well as being thrown into prison. You have to admire them. They went through some tough times for our benefit."

But the question of which political party to vote for was raised. Where would I start? It would be like trying to find the right religion all over again – I'd have to find out what each one's manifesto was, check out their activities, their representatives, their successes and failures. I had more than enough to do finding my feet, finding out which planet I was on, what I wanted in my life, where I belonged.

But did I really need to belong anywhere? Be part of a group, be a member with responsibilities? My 'membership' with the Witnesses was conditional – as long as I respected their rules and toed the line I could stay and enjoy the benefits. Disobey the rules and you're out. Any club would be the same no doubt. I considered that maybe that's all the Witnesses were, just a club? Understandable, I suppose, but there was just one difference. I'm sure that no other club would instruct its remaining members to ostracise the one who had been removed. Big difference. Huge!

No, politics would have to wait. I'd have to put it to the back of my mind until there was space in my head and time in my week to devote to the subject. It was getting to be tiresome, all these important decisions to make. I just wanted to enjoy my life and not have to worry about such heavy issues anymore.

It was time I gave mum a ring. See if she was all right.

As usual our conversation felt a bit forced, laboured. It was like that face to face as well, to be honest. Mum was a very private person and her practice of not letting others see the 'real' Marianne extended to her daughter too. It always felt as if she was holding something back. But we chatted for a while about the meetings and whether she was getting a lift home each time. Whether there were enough people out on the ministry, and if there was always someone to work along with. It was rare that any of the Witnesses went out from door to door on their own but mum had been known to do that once or twice. I didn't think it was a safe thing to do but mum was confident of God's protection, so who was I to argue with her?

I enquired about her medication and if she'd been low recently. She assured me she was up to date with her prescriptions and, no, her mood had been quite stable lately, and there's really nothing to worry about. I had to take her word for it. In a congregation of about a hundred people there was no one I felt I could ring to ask if they would look in on mum from time to time. I shouldn't have to ask anyway. They were, reportedly, such a loving, caring congregation of Brothers and Sisters, I should have been able to trust that someone, somehow was keeping a bit of an eye on her.

She asked about my job, whether living at Esther's was still working out all right. She didn't ask about Will. She never mentioned him when we spoke on the phone, ever. I didn't want to talk about my life to mum. I knew she didn't approve of me not attending meetings anymore, of leaving the Truth. I knew that she would fully expect me to be killed when Armageddon comes. I had rejected God and his earthly organisation. There was no hope for me.

Now I'd been out of the Witnesses' clutches for some time, I could see how tight their grip had been on me and how trapped my mother actually still was. She didn't know it, didn't realise that there was a way out. I suppose it was her security blanket and provided some stability in her life. But surely there were other ways to fulfil those needs without giving up her freedom of choice, without having to sacrifice her interests and skills, without, at times, having to give up her family.

Our conversation drew to a close with both of us promising to call again soon. Yes, I would try and come up to visit before the end of the summer. And she told me I should try and talk to Peter again. But I won't, I know that. He clearly does not want to interact with me, not on a personal level anyway. We needed to keep the lines open with regard to mum's health but as soon as we'd covered that, there was nothing else to discuss, or so it appeared. He had been made a Ministerial Servant the previous year, a position of responsibility in the congregation, and had to be seen to be doing everything by the book, so socialising (albeit on the phone) with his now 'worldly' sister was definitely out. What could I do? I had to accept it. Maybe he'd grow up one day, even get to know Will. Funnily enough, they'd get on really well, I felt.

The south coast was heating up as July approached. The whole town was extremely busy with holiday makers sauntering along in the heat in their sun hats and shades. Ice cream and candy floss sellers were dotted along the three-mile length of the promenade, the odd dropped cone melting in the sun surrounded by hungry pigeons pecking at the sogginess. Out at sea the sun sparkled on the water, jewel-like in its brilliance, and the waves gently lapped against the sturdy groins soaking the dark wood yet again.

I wandered up Terminus Road from the Post Office at the other end as I needed to put some of my wages into my account. Feeling a sudden urge to see the sea had become quite regular and on many occasions I'd found myself having walked miles along the shore from home right up to the pier. The openness of the water appealed to me. It almost called to me and my relationship with the water, swimming in it almost every day, was strong and sure. The sea would always be there. Never would I wake up one morning to find it had gone.

As I walked I could suddenly smell chips. Vinegar and hot fat. When Peter and I were kids, chips were our treat after a Thursday night meeting, but only on the weeks when mum could afford it. There was always a hurry to get served across the counter before our bus home turned the corner. If we missed it, we'd have to wait another half an hour. I viewed the steaming food wrapped in newspaper as our reward for sitting through the meeting and, on the nights when we didn't visit the chip shop, I couldn't wait to get home and put some bread under the grill. Such deep concentration on serious issues always produced a rumbling stomach. I felt ravenous now and made my way along to the pier entrance for a bag of those slimy golden sticks.

I couldn't say I'd been searching hard for a new job but I occasionally glanced in the Eastbourne Herald at the situations vacant just to see what kind of opportunities were out there. I loved my job at the Beefeater although it was so hard on my feet. The late nights were all right but I was getting a little fed up with such unsocial hours. Many times, Sandy and Ellie had asked me to go out with them but I had to decline because of work. Esther pointed out one particular job which she thought would be within my capabilities. It was a basic office junior job – filing, typing, opening the mail, that kind of thing. Of course, I had no other qualifications except a few O' Levels. Maybe that would be sufficient for an employer to consider me.

"You can also prove you're reliable, trustworthy and diligent. Mark would give you a glowing reference, I'm sure. Why don't you go for it? Just give them a ring. You've got nothing to lose." Esther was always looking out for me, she was wonderful. I rang and was offered an interview the following day. During the lengthy interview the manager, Mr Roades, explained that although he'd advertised for a junior he didn't really want a 16 year-old fresh out of school. Wanted someone with a little more experience and who would be willing to train. I felt he was a bit nosey, but it all ended well when he offered me the job to start whenever I'd worked my notice at the restaurant.

I was thrilled! There was, however, one downside. The business was the insurance company that Sandy also worked for. I wondered if all the office staff knew what she was. I'd suspected it was where she worked from the moment I'd seen the advert but told myself I'd just have to deal with it somehow if I actually got the job. It was simple in my mind – if she stays down one end of the office and I'm at the other, we should all get along just fine. I could be civil to her, no problem, but I wouldn't be able to socialise with her outside of office hours.

"Don't be stupid," remarked Will. He congratulated me on getting the job but then when I explained it would be in the same office as Sandy he tore into me.

"Think about it, Jess. Sandy and Ellie used to be your friends. They haven't changed. They were gay when you met them, they're still gay." This was the first time I'd seen him even a little bit angry. "Look at your attitude and tell me honestly, do you really want to cut them out of your life so completely? Don't consider whether you *should*, think about if that's really what you *want*. Come on, you've felt how painful it is to be ostracised. Hurts doesn't it? And now that's exactly what you're doing to them."

Oh God!! I'd hit that brick wall again. The one that's only built with black or white bricks. This or that, right or wrong, no in between. I'd love to break it down, take a hammer to each and every brick and make a pile of dust out of the lot of them, and watch it being blown away in the wind. I think I need some help, need to talk it through with someone that understands - an insider - but how would I find one that wouldn't judge me? Or one that wouldn't go running to the Elders to report me. The fact that I wasn't going to meetings and not associating with any Witnesses did not make me feel any less fearful. I couldn't shake off my worries that at some point my actions would be thrown before me, that I'd be made to account for everything I did, made to answer to the Elders again.

Damn it, Will was right yet again – Will, the sensible one. The stable, level-headed one in our relationship. Yes, he had a few years on me and a sensitive mother who had taught him well. Up to now there had never been an occasion when it had been me giving advice to Will, always the other way round. I felt like a burden, with my weird opinions and odd ways. Felt as if I needed to be sorted out all the time. I felt like a child.

Did he ever get fed up with me? Wouldn't he have preferred a normal girlfriend, one that didn't keep surprising him, one that he didn't have to keep correcting when yet another conscience issue arose? I put my fears to him and, fighting with my emotions and hold back my tears, said I'd understand if he felt I was no fun, that I was too serious about life. I lied and said it would be ok if he wanted us to be just friends, that I didn't expect him to look after me all the time and talk sense into me at every turn. The truth was, I don't know what I'd do without him. I needed him by my side. Would he wait for me?

I would get there, I knew I would. I accepted it would take some time, Will had pointed that out to me and he was right. I just hoped he would still be with me at the end of it all. Would I ever get to a position where I could consider myself 'normal'? I didn't have the memories that other people my age had – pulling Christmas crackers; the excitement of opening presents; sending invitations out for my own or attending a friend's birthday party; cracking open large Easter eggs; the boredom of school assemblies; sending unsigned Valentine's cards, or receiving them; bonding with classmates on school camping trips; dancing at a 5th year disco; the thrill of being asked out on a date; the opportunity to stay on at school and learn a skill. These were things that brought people together, where friendships were made. Shared memories of fun times. They didn't exist in my world. I had no anchor. I felt like an alien.

He told me he loved me. He told me often, and I needed that reassurance. Needed to know he was nearby all the time, in spirit if not physically. A sounding board, a confidante, a partner in life with whom to share new experiences. He reminded me that this is exactly how he felt about me too. He recounted the time I'd sat and listened to him rattle on about his difficult clients and having to chase their payments, about an issue he'd had with an old friend who'd turned up asking for money, the aches and pains after that particularly long journey following a lengthy atmospheric moonlight shoot far up on the east coast. He reminded me that I was there for him too.

His words sprang to mind whenever I felt a slight pang of insecurity: "We're a team, you and me, Jess. I want you in my life regardless of who you've been, or who you think you'll become. I *love* you."

I didn't deserve him, I really didn't.

About a couple of weeks after I'd moved down over a year ago Esther had whispered in my ear:

"Want to have a little chat with you sometime."

Her tone suggested secrecy, so I didn't mention it to Will. It took place the following day when we found a mutually convenient time to sit at the kitchen table. Esther offered me a Lift lemon tea which I quickly declined. Mum had drunk that disgusting stuff throughout the seventies.

She came straight out with it, no messing around: "Jess, you need to be thinking about some proper birth control. I know it's the responsibility of both of you, but it would be wise for you to start taking the Pill." She paused. "I'm sure you mum has had this chat with you before, but I thought I'd just remind you, now that you're in a proper relationship and all that."

She hadn't put me under any pressure to confirm or deny that Will and I were having an active sex life, she just said what needed to be said and didn't wait for any kind of response. She blew on her teacup as she held it carefully with both hands. That stuff stayed hot for days.

"Well, it may surprise you, Esther, but no, I've never had any conversation like this with my mum. She's not open to discussing personal things and in her eyes, unless I'm married, the only form of contraception is abstinence. Simple. That's how she sees things. She would never discuss the ins and outs of something I shouldn't be doing anyway."

I'd heard of the Pill: a girl had mentioned it at the eyewear manufacturer's where I worked previously. Said she'd forgotten to take it for the last few days and was now worried if her next period would start.

So, Esther's advice was followed up by attending a doctor's appointment and being prescribed the said tablets. I felt highly embarrassed throughout the whole process and the wait at the chemist's for them to prepare my order was excruciating. No one could possibly have known what was written on the sheet that I handed over the counter but I was just dreading someone I knew coming through the door. I was sure they would have been able to tell just by the look of guilt on my face.

Marriage, and sex outside of it, had always been one of the issues I'd questioned. Inwardly, of course, it wouldn't have gone down very well to vocalise these doubts. From my early teens I'd wondered why Adam and Eve hadn't got married. There was no mention in the book of Genesis of Eve having a hard time choosing her wedding dress, no word about a three-tiered cake, the exchanging of rings, a ceremony conducted by an Elder, a following reception - maybe with some wine. But the couple had obviously had sex because they'd had kids. So, what's the story with all these wedding practices we have today? And why is it wrong for two people in love and committed to each other to have sex without first getting a certificate? It was just one of those rules that didn't make sense. I was aware it wasn't just a Witness rule, the Catholics had it too. So, whilst I felt at ease with my relationship with Will, I was still looking over my shoulder and my guilty conscience rumbled away a little louder on some days. Like the day I picked up that first prescription.

Now, a year or so later, it was time to collect it again. This time I would get a six-month supply instead of collecting every two months. Good. A whole year's supply would be even better. Or maybe they could just give me five years' worth, that would be perfect.

The bell dinged as I entered the chemist's on the high street, that nauseating hospital smell filling my nostrils immediately. There were only two customers in front of me and I got served pretty quick. I moved to the side and waited for my name to be called. One of the ladies, sitting on the only chair available, looked up and smiled at me. I recognised her from the newsagent's where she worked. It was a small village really and I was starting to feel part of the community, each of these little nods of recognition confirming it in a small way.

The door opened, I shuffled away from it, and in walked Ginny Peacock.

Please God, not now, I thought.

"Jess, how lovely to see you! Just let me hand this in, then we can have a chat."

Take your time.

"Ah, so how are you? We've seen you quite a few times now, here and abouts. Are you back down here permanently, then?"

There was no escaping her enquiries this time. I was trapped between the busybody and the incontinence pads.

"Hi Ginny. Yes, I think you know where I live now."

"Yes, well, we moved over from Old Town about six months ago. It's so lovely out here, so fresh. Is that your boyfriend we see you with sometimes?"

She didn't mess around. This would be a prime piece of gossip for any Jehovah's Witness – a baptised member being seen walking hand in hand with a worldly man. I wondered what she would do with the information. I mean, I wasn't attending meetings or associating with any Witnesses and therefore I would not be a threat. So, it shouldn't do any harm to confirm that she was right.

"Yes, that's Will. He's a lovely man. We've known each other about three years now."

"Ah, that's sweet, it's so nice to hear romance isn't dead."

It would be if the Witnesses had their way. At almost every meeting there was some warning about dating a member of the opposite sex with reminders of the consequences should a couple mess up and end up sleeping together. They run the very real risk of being publicly reproved from the platform in front of the whole congregation, or, if they were judged to be unrepentant, disfellowshipped and cut off from their friends and families. Chaprones sprung into action at the slightest whiff of attraction and there were strict rules for courting couples – no hand holding or even sitting next to each other in the Kingdom Hall unless you were officially engaged. And if an engagement was called off the couple had to have a meeting with the Elders to establish the reasons. That promise to marry was as serious as getting married itself and a break-up was treated as highly suspicious. I don't know how anyone actually had a successful, happy courtship. How could a couple be alone long enough to build a close relationship, to have private conversations, to just relax in each other's company?

"Do you think you'll get married soon, then?"

I could see what she was up to. Dig, dig, dig. Luckily my name was called and I was saved from having to lay my life out on the table for her to scrutinise and spread around. If she only knew what I was holding in my hand.

But it was private. My life was just that – MY life. No one else's business. The concept of privacy didn't seem to exist within the Organisation. Everyone knew who was doing what and with whom and where they were going and when and how long for. Yes, friends know these things about each other, that's true, but people's activities were discussed and assessed no matter who they were. And the judgement followed, naturally. It was unhealthy to say the least.

I felt sad leaving the Beefeater. Mark and the team had been good to me and such fun to work with. I told them I'd never forget them and would come and have a meal sometimes. On my last shift they gathered at the door and presented me with a gorgeous bunch of flowers and an envelope containing a card signed by everyone. That brought tears to my eyes.

I'd learned a lot during my time at the restaurant, not least how to deal with members of the public, and many other skills that I could take to my new role as Office Junior at Hepworth Insurance. The first week went by quickly as I took in the office lay out and met my colleagues and listened as each one ran through their role. They explained how their work would create jobs for me to do and how that fitted into the whole operation. It was fascinating. After a couple of weeks of filing paperwork, making the tea, replenishing stock cupboards and opening the post my supervisor started me on the hard stuff.

Cover notes. Now this was getting interesting. I was handed a stack of quadruplicate pads and set up on a desk towards the back of the office, right at the other end to Sandy, as I'd hoped. Dominic, who been with the company for a couple of years, was assigned to help me get to grips with the task and his way of explaining things was, let's say, economic. But I got there and felt that I'd been entrusted with something really important. These sheets were legal documents and had to be completed, distributed and stored accurately. I suddenly felt I had a real job. Dominic complimented me on my work and the speed at which I'd picked it up. He sweetly apologised for not being a very good teacher, that Mr Roades always gave him such tasks, probably hoping he'd improve. He seemed quite nice, had a twinkle in his eye, but the only thing was, he stood a little too close. I could smell his deodorant.

The boss said I could wear what I like to work as long as it was smart and reflected the high standards of the company. Fair enough. So, I bought a classy pair of navy trousers and a floral blouse or two. I still didn't want to wear a skirt – I just knew it would feel too much like I was going to a meeting. I felt comfortable in trousers and didn't have to worry about wearing a slip or tights. Or wonder how my legs were positioned should anyone look under the desk.

Sandy acknowledged me everyday as I arrived and I did the same to her. It didn't cost anything to be civil. I missed the girls, really I did, but best to keep some distance. My conscience had taken a battering over the last few years, I needed to avoid anything that was going to make it bother me, and Sandy's living arrangement with Ellie was something that would.

One day, midweek, Sandy wasn't there when I came through the door. Whenever anyone was planning to be off they would write it in the diary. So, after checking the book, seeing there was no entry from Sandy, I asked Tina if she'd rung in.

There'd been no word from her. Ten o'clock came, ten thirty. Someone tried her phone but there was no answer. It was a bit worrying, she was never late for work.

Finally, at half past eleven the door opened and in walked Sandy looking, quite frankly, like shit. Like she hadn't slept all night. Her hair was messy and black circles sat underneath her eyes. I walked towards the kitchen area and I gave her a moment to settle herself at her desk. Should I ask if she was all right? I'd made the decision to avoid her. Would I be backtracking, letting myself down, if I now showed concern for her and talked to her like nothing had changed, like she hadn't told me they were lesbians?

I stood at the counter waiting for the kettle to boil and took a moment to glance in her direction. From this distance I could see her puffy eyes on a face she wouldn't raise. The scrunched tissue in her fist she reached down and replaced with a clean one from the box. What on earth had happened? In a split second my heart went out to her. Whatever it was, she was suffering and I wanted to comfort her. I threw the teaspoon down and made my way towards her with my arms reaching out. As I neared, she knew my presence, stood up and matched the shape of my affection.

How could I not comfort her? How could I leave her to cry and not be a friend to her? It felt inhumane and I couldn't do it.

I didn't speak to her or try to get her to talk. I just let her cry on my shoulder. The others looked on in sympathy, someone made and brought that cup of tea for her. Over her shoulder the Manager caught my eye and indicated with a nod of his head that I should take her to the ladies' room. There, she explained that Ellie had been involved in a car accident that morning. The driver had mounted the kerb on a tight corner and had run into her knocking her to the ground. He then proceeded to drive over her leg and zoomed away down the road. Some bright person took down the registration number and the Police were now informed.

"Oh my goodness, Sandy, you shouldn't have come in today. You need to go back to the hospital to be with Ellie. The boss'll understand."

"I'd rather be here, Jess. I'm better when I'm busy. Ellie's stable and being looked after. Anyway, it's so nice to see you. I've missed you, you silly cow." She laughed a bit, and gave me a friendly punch on the shoulder.

I owed Sandy and Ellie an explanation and a massive apology. I hoped they would understand and try to see it from my point of view. I didn't know them well enough to tell if either was spiritually minded; we'd never had anything remotely like an in-depth, heartfelt conversation about the deeper things of the universe. Our chatter was usually about work, clothes, going out, music, people we came across, that kind of thing. So, I decided that when the time was right I'd do my best to explain. Sandy left work early and went back to the hospital and I said I'd call her later on that evening to see how the patient was. The news wasn't good. She would need surgery on her lower leg followed by extensive physiotherapy and a lot of patience. Poor thing.

The events of the day reminded me of the time I was left alone while in great pain. How hurtful that felt. At a meeting during the year that I was disfellowshipped, I fell hard on the icy steps outside the Kingdom Hall after a meeting. As I gasped in agony at my twisted ankle I heard footsteps behind, glad that someone was coming to help me. But they walked straight past. In fact, several people carried on walking, ignoring my moans of pain, and got into their comfortable cars to make the journey home. It took me an hour to do the twenty-minute walk into town to catch the bus home and many cars passed me along the way. Nobody was prepared to break the rule of not talking to a disfellowshipped person, even human decency and normal human instinct to help was denied. "That's not right," I told myself at the time, but I accepted it in a strange way - it was part of my punishment.

No doubt those Witnesses that had left me on the icy ground sobbing in pain, the ones who had walked and driven past me, were very pleased with themselves, satisfied that they had stayed faithful and had ignored a sinner as instructed. I bet they all slept well that night.

But I didn't want to be that type of person and couldn't see how that would ever be the right thing to do, not under any circumstances. I let myself imagine, for a moment, that I still believed in Jesus Christ and recalled from my Bible education that he had not been known to act in that way. No matter who the person was, whatever the situation, when someone was in need he helped them. And he instructed others to show loving kindness and do the same. So how had the Jehovah's Witnesses messed up so badly with that one?

A few weeks later Ellie was well enough to come along to the staff meal, albeit in a wheelchair. Business had been good lately with several new clients accepting their quotes, so Mr Roades had treated us to a night out at one of the best Indian restaurants in town. The food was delicious and, as it was buffet style, I had the chance to try dishes I would never have ordered. My adventurousness didn't usually stretch beyond chicken korma.

At the restaurant, seated in between Sandy and Dominic, I had to admit that I felt quite comfortable surrounded by 'worldly' people, though by now, I was using that judgmental phrase less and less. They were my friends, colleagues and mates. That huge myth – in fact, that massive lie, that all non-Witnesses were evil - had been well and truly exposed for me and the injustice permanently removed from my thoughts. Yes, there would still be some bad people around, so caution was wise in some circumstances. It was all about balance and making choices.

Dominic kept flashing me his sparkly-eyed look and each time it felt as though he was about to say something. He never did, though. At one point, when heads were turned towards the waiter bringing the food, I felt the back of his hand against my thigh. I quickly moved my leg as if it was on fire. *He can pack that in,* I thought. How cheeky! He knows I have a boyfriend as Will had picked me up from work one day on his way through town. Dominic had offered him a seat while I finished tidying my desk. So what was his game?

I managed to force a final forkful in my mouth and, holding my hands up, declared that I was fit to burst. No, I don't think I could eat a dessert, but coffee would be nice. We all placed our drinks orders with the waiter.

I'd just dropped my scrunched-up napkin on my plate when I felt a lingering warmth on my thigh. Dominic! This time he actually put his hand on my leg and squeezed it. And he left it there despite me having jiggled my leg; he probably thought I was enjoying his touch. There was nowhere to go but somehow I had to give him the message to remove it, and quickly. The coffee arrived but I noticed there were no teaspoons with the sugar bowl. I had to use a dessert spoon and, dipping it in my hot drink, I stirred in the sugar. I took my time, got it nice and hot, imagined the expansion of the metal to create a larger surface area. With that spoon pressed hard on the back of his hand he yelped suddenly, rushing off in the direction of the gents. Someone remarked on his urgency and suggested the food was going right through him. On his return they teased him and asked him how his stomach was. As he played reluctantly along with their banter I noticed his shirt cuff was wet. He kept his wandering hand to himself for the rest of the evening.

That was another mother and daughter lesson that had never taken place; rejecting unwanted male attention. Not a subject that was taught at home, though all the advice anyone could possibly want was in the magazines or the Youth Book.* But the hot spoon method seemed to work quite well. He was in the car when Sandy gave me a lift home. I sat next to Ellie in the back and wondered if I should perhaps tell someone about his wandering hand. As I got out of the car I said goodbye to the girls, and to Dominic. I shot him my best 'warning' look but the one he gave back to me was on a different level. In that second, I could see his sparkling eyes had turned into something dark as he fired the most piercing look into my eyes. His flat "Goodbye Jessica" had an undertone that quite unnerved me.

CHAPTER 5

It was Saturday. I hadn't been swimming for a few days. Not in the Leisure Pool anyway. Will said he was coming over later so I had time to go to the pool. My sea swims were great; invigorating in a way that only icy cold water could be, but the muscle exercise and build up of stamina came from doing lengths. Back and forth, front crawl and breast-stroke, with a few on my back. By the end of a session it always felt as if I'd had a really good full-body workout.

I towel dried my hair and gave it a quick brush through. I usually let it dry naturally, that way the curls would form nicely. On my way out I bumped into Theresa who'd just finished her shift. I always seemed to catch her as she was signing out at the front desk. She told me about a new charity swimming challenge that was coming up, which was just one among many fundraising initiatives following on from Live Aid.

"Live Aid?" I had no idea what she was on about.

"Yes, you know, Live Aid, Bob Geldof, "Give us your focking money"?" She laughed out loud at her own impression.

"Ummm, nope. What's Live Aid?"

It seems the biggest charity music event of the century, which took place two years ago, had completely passed me by. Theresa told me that it was one of the largest satellite link-ups and television broadcasts of all time; a huge audience in 150 countries around the world watched the live coverage and, through donations and pledges, around £150 million was raised for the famine in Ethiopia. These continuing sports challenges would keep it running, keep the money coming in.

Had I been asleep? How did I not know about this? So, 1985, July, what was I doing? I had to think hard and work it out. The date of my disfellowshipping had stuck firmly in my mind, 1st October 1984, and I placed events as either PD (pre-disfellowshipped or AR (after reinstatement). So it happened while I was out in the cold, while I was working at the eyewear manufacturers, swimming and being thoroughly lonely and depressed. And, of course, attending the Thursday night and Sunday morning meetings. I rarely watched TV at that time. I was just surviving and not really enjoying anything in life. In any case, there wasn't much on the box that Witnesses could legitimately watch without feeling guilty. Without assessing whether they would still watch it if Jesus himself was in the room. There wasn't much that didn't contain some immoral couple having an extra-marital affair, gratuitous violence, spiritism, the occult. I was trying to be the best Witness I could be and kept myself away from worldly influences, even if it was only on TV, and so this massive event that the whole world knew about had escaped me.

It would have been interesting to know what was going on. It might have been good to watch, even on our black and white portable. I recalled the few glimpses I'd caught of Michael Buerke's horrifying news report on the BBC. It caught my attention because he had described the scenes of famine as 'biblical'. I'd changed the channel. I couldn't bear to watch it. I hadn't realised that something as huge as Live Aid had come directly from that report.

Starvation and poverty was one of those subjects that was easy to dismiss as a Witness. There had never been any encouragement to donate to charity. Nothing from the platform, nothing in the Watchtower or Awake magazines and it was certainly never discussed. The answer to people's suffering lay in them receiving the Good News of God's Kingdom. That's all they needed. And so, on a local level, the help that came from JWs stopped at the offer of a Bible study. If that was rejected, then there was no hope for them; they would never get themselves out of their predicament. As for everyone else around the world who was starving, God would sort it out in his own time. Hardly a satisfying solution; to be happy to let people starve knowing that God will end all their suffering soon, watch them die in agony but then resurrect them, give them another chance. I always wondered, what about NOW?

I thought about Jesus' parable of the Good Samaritan. The Jewish traveller who had been beaten and left for dead needed help. After a Jewish Priest and then a Levite had stepped over him, ignoring his suffering, a Samaritan bandaged his wounds, gave him a lift on his donkey to an inn. At his own expense, this kind stranger made sure the man was looked after and given a good meal and anything else he needed. Again, it was clear to me that some of the instruction, or lack of it in this case, from the Governing Body, regarding people in physical need, was wrong.

"Yeh, count me in." I didn't hesitate when Theresa explained what I'd need to do to get sponsors and promote this challenge. This felt like something really worthwhile. I felt needed all of a sudden. I could raise money to help local people, my neighbours. Me! I could actually do some good! I got the sponsor form from the reception desk and set about getting people to sign up – anything, 50p, 75p, £1 would be fantastic, thank you. This felt good.

As I walked home along the beach path I wondered if that Live Aid concert would be repeated on TV any time. Theresa said it went on for 16 hours with performances from, among many others, David Bowie, the Boomtown Rats, Elvis Costello and Queen. Charles and Diana were in the audience. I bet they loved it. I SO wished I'd known it was on.

Along the path back home at the point where the housing stopped I heard steady footsteps behind me, almost in time with my own. I don't know why they should have caught my attention as there were several people using the path. It was just a strange feeling I had. I tested out my suspected follower and I stopped to fumble for something imaginary in my bag. True enough, they stopped too. I glanced back to see a woman in a long black coat and a floppy cap. She'd let her dog off the lead and was watching it sniffing in amongst the sea campion. I told myself off for being too jumpy and carried on home.

It had been an intense week at work with lots of new business being written and after a long evening swim I really felt I could do with a good night out. I needed to let my hair down, go dancing, get a takeaway, anything. I phoned the girls to see what they were up to later on. Sadly, they already had plans for tonight but were up for it next Saturday. Ellie would still have to be careful but she wanted to go, even if she couldn't dance.

I'd been thinking of having a new hairstyle. There was a woman who got on the same bus as me every day who had pink hair and it made me consider my own locks. Something short and spikey, like Madonna. I could do whatever I wanted with my hair now. It was my choice. Should I go purple? Green? Perhaps a pale blue with black ends. I spent the afternoon in WH Smith's pouring through the women's magazines hoping for some inspiration. I was too old for Seventeen now, and Prima was all about crafts. A flick through Women's World revealed that if I entered a free draw I could win a 'Fantastic Fitted Kitchen!' The knitting pattern in Woman's Realm for a lacy bed jacket was really not calling to me but further down the front cover was an article entitled 'Happy New Hairdos'. I turned to the cited page but was faced with five women who looked as if they were on their way to a JW meeting. No thank you.

My old favourite – Smash Hits – was beckoning to me down the other end of the shelf. The centre pages were a poster of Toyah and as I looked into her heavily-lined eyes I knew I'd found my new look. It was as easy as that!

That night, after a fish and chips supper with Will and a couple of drinks at the Castle Inn, we relaxed on the settee with a bottle of wine and some chocolate. Esther was out at her friend's, so we were free to put some records on and crank up the volume. Will loved his music and was extremely knowledgeable about bands, their members and how they'd been formed. He'd been to small venues when his work had taken him up to London and told me funny stories of accidents on stage, singer's late arrivals and equipment not working. It sounded so exciting, and I begged him to take me up to the city sometime. I wanted to experience a real London club, with bouncers on the door and spotlights on the stairs. He didn't answer my request.

He proceeded to tell me about the drugs scene where deals were done openly at the bar. About drinks being spiked, girls out cold on the toilet floor and fights breaking out. Groups of girls tottering away at club closing time being followed by a taxi driver hoping to pick off one of the gullible ones for a quickie on the back seat.

This was the real world. I'd be ok. I wouldn't get involved in any of that kind of thing, and I'd be with Will. He'd look after me. What was the problem? If it was ok for him to go, why not take me? We'd have a great time!

I considered telling Will of my plan for a new look but decided it would be better to surprise him. I didn't tell the girls either. Saturday was the day. My hair appointment was in town straight after my morning swim. I'd been to the salon earlier in the week for a strand test and to discuss which shade I wanted. It was all so exciting! I felt so grown-up and in charge of my own life. My money was my own, so was my hair and no-one had the right to tell me what to do. As I sat in the pumped up chair I imagined I could feel the bold shade I'd chosen taking a firm hold on every single strand of hair, sucking up the colour, being renewed, reinvented. The finished result was exactly how I'd wanted it; spikey on the top, graduating down. I'd kept the shoulder length and somehow the hairdresser had made it dead straight. The colour? An orangey red. Bright and cheerful. I was so pleased with my reflection, and I couldn't wait to show it off.

My step was springy as I walked through town towards the clothes shops. I held my head high and strutted along the pavement wearing a private smile. A few people looked at my hair and smiled. Outside the bank I spotted, of all people, Ginny Peacock. I made eye contact with her but she clearly didn't recognise me! *Result!* I thought.

So now, I needed a whole new outfit to go with my new hair. With Toyah as my inspiration, I went for black, bold and daring. She was a sight to see, a bit scary and quite different to any other artist. I found a dress that reflected her style and tried it on for size. Black and shiny, it was short - way above the knee – with one long sleeve and the other shoulder quite bare. The top was a kind of wrapped piece which let my midriff exposed. I found an extra-long narrow belt with studs which looked great wrapped twice around my hips so that went in my bag too. Fishnet tights were called for and a pair of biker boots which rose half-way up my legs. The straps and laces and rivets in the boots were matched in the leather cuff I found in another shop. A large pair of gold disc earrings and my outfit was almost complete. It had almost wiped me out of money for the week but I was determined this outfit was going to get a lot of use. It was worth it.

"When the girls arrive, Will, ask them to come in the house for a minute would you?" I shouted my request to him through the bedroom door.

"No, you can't come in. I've… I've done something different. You'll see later."

I wanted all three of them together to see the new me. Dark smoky eyes, another coat of black nail polish, a dusting of glitter body spray on my middle and I was ready to go downstairs. I clomped down, one step at a time as my skirt was too tight, and stood before them.

I heard gasps, giggles, and then silence. Esther had joined the audience and stood there actually, literally with her mouth open.

"Well, how d'you like my new look, people?" I turned around so they could get the full effect.

"Fuck me!" said Will, eventually.

"Bloody hell!" said Esther.

"You'd better watch your back tonight," came advice from Sandy.

Ellie remained silent, looking me up and down.

"Yeh, suits you. Good on ya, girl," she finally said, with her head nodding in approval.

It was still light at nine when we 'walked the plank', down the length of the pier and in through the double doors to Dixieland. Warm too. No need for a jacket. The girls had made their own way there and had got a table for us. Unfortunately, Dominic was also there, perched on a chair facing backwards, dragging on a cigarette. He gave me a cold look as he said hello and swung his chair round the right way.

I asked Will if I could borrow a fiver to get some drinks and promised to pay him back out of next week's pay packet. Five pounds would get me just enough alcohol to relax and enjoy myself, but not enough to get too drunk. I'd learned my lesson after last time. It was going to be a perfect night.

DJ Spinney was on holiday so there was someone by the name of DJ Guest doing the tricks tonight. His music was heavier than Spinney. More base. In the Funky Corner, an area by the small bar, a number of people had gathered, and, so Will told me, these were the people in the know about music. They kept up with all the new dance sounds, both here and in America, and talked about house music from Chicago, Detroit techno and a new up and coming sound – rave. They sometimes brought records with them and got the DJ to play them to see what the crowd thought.

DJ Guest (was that really his name or was he just a guest DJ?) played one track that was so brilliant, almost hypnotic. It got everyone on the dancefloor, showing off their practiced moves. Sandy was near me as we did our own thing to the beat. Whenever I got up to dance Dominic wasn't far away, either. He didn't talk to me which was fine, but he kept looking at me, but he never smiled. I couldn't work him out. I bobbed over to the DJ and indicated for him to play that record again. Of course, that's something that a good DJ would never do, but I didn't know that.

"Later," he shouted. "Go and talk to the guys in the Funky Corner. They might have some more new stuff." I could barely hear him over the music but got the gist. So, I got talking to them and had a look through the small collection of records they'd brought along. None of the artists I knew but logged them in my memory.

"What was that record that was on just now?" I asked one of the group.

"Good Life by Inner City," Jacks shouted to me. "Fucking good mix," he said as he took a drag on his cigarette. "You look fantastic," he said as his eyes took in my shape from top to bottom and sideways. "Wanna dance?"

"Nah, I'll get back to my friends. Thanks, cheers."

I headed back over to Sandy. No drinks were allowed on the dancefloor, so we stood by a tall table and bobbed along to the heavy base. Across the hall, Ellie was carefully making her way back from the toilets. She'd become fiercely independent, not wanting any support from anyone. She needed to get her strength back and the only way she'd do it was by carrying her own weight.

"Ey up, look who's coming," announced Sandy, looking over my shoulder. It was Jacks. "Wanker. Thinks he knows it all. Takes it all too seriously. Pisshead."

"You don't like him then?" She didn't get my irony and just sneered as he came nearer. Next thing I knew she'd downed her drink, and then mine and, grabbing me by the hand pulled me into the middle of the dancefloor. I let myself get into the groove (although maybe that term was out of date now that disco was a thing of the past). All I could hear was the music and all I could feel was the beat. My feet did the work, my body just followed and as I closed my eyes I floated on a wave of happiness rooted in freedom.

I didn't feel out of place there with my orangey-red hair. There were several who were dressed like Boy George, other guys in suits and dark glasses. Some I really couldn't tell if they were male or female, but I concluded it didn't really matter. It was funny dancing in heavy boots instead of stilettos. Much more comfortable, but one of my heels was beginning to rub. Will was around somewhere, we didn't stay glued together. There was no need. He'd been coming here for years so he knew a lot of the people and spent more time talking, or rather shouting, than dancing. We hooked up at the bar or on the dance floor throughout the night and, of course, always got together for the final slow dance before heading home.

I checked in my bag that I'd put a plaster in (just in case, you never know with new footwear) and headed for a bit of privacy in the toilets. Ugh! Yes, a blister was forming. Plaster secured, I made my way back along the dimly lit corridor. Suddenly, out of nowhere, I was face to face with Jacks.

"Come on, love. Have a little dance with me. You know you want to." He was drunk and took a long drag of his cigarette, blowing the smoke up above him.

He got closer and pushed me up against the wall and I could feel his chest against mine. His breath was foul and I turned my head away. I didn't feel scared, more disgusted. I knew that I only needed to let out a sharp scream and someone would come to my rescue, but in a weird way I wanted to manage the situation by myself.

My groin kneeing skills had been used before and it crossed my mind to use them again. It would be so easy, but I didn't want to make a scene. I could have headbutted him. A short, sharp crack on the nose. No.

One of his hands was on my shoulder, the other making its way up the back of my skirt, all the time his breath was in my face, and he tried to kiss me. Dirty bastard. I turned my face away. What makes him think he's got the right to lay his hands on me?

"Let go," I said plainly and firmly to him, with my head raised, looking him straight in the eye.

"What did you say, "let's go"?" He gave a dirty laugh. "Let's go where, eh, shall we go outside for a bit?"

"I said, let go." Second warning.

I felt his fingers scrabbling around trying to rip a hole in my fishnets.

"Are you gonna actually let go or not?"

Not, it seemed. His strength was increasing and I could feel the roughness of the painted woodchip wallpaper through the back of my top.

I reached down to his trousers. Felt around for a warm area at the front where there was a little swollen thing. As I grabbed it and squeezed, the noise he made, I thought, would have been enough to alert someone. I squeezed harder and his legs started to buckle and his grip on me loosen. I kept on tightening my fingers around his little package and by now he was shorter than me. He actually, literally begged me to stop!

"Let go," he whispered.

"What was that? "Let go," did you say?" He nodded his head, a sweat had broken out on his forehead.

"Let go, pleeease."

"I think you need to apologise to me, don't you?"

"I'm sorry."

"Didn't hear you."

"I'm sorry!" he shouted as I released my grip and he slumped to the floor holding himself. I stepped over him. I momentarily considered booting him in the balls – these boots would make a good job of that – but instead I straightened my skirt and checked my tights and made my way to the bar.

It wasn't until I was standing there waiting to be served that I realised I was shaking.

"Brandy, please." This one was for medicinal purposes. It didn't count.

I sat on the high stool at the bar and felt myself calming down as the golden liquid ran through my body. There was a guy in leather standing in front of me, holding out a fiver for his drinks. As I put my glass down he offered to buy me another.

"No, thanks." I peered around me, tried to see where the others were.

"Oh, go on, just a small one." I'd had enough.

"Don't you men listen? I said NO! Now fuck off!"

As I stomped away I noticed Dominic standing over by the Funky Corner. He was talking to Jacks, pointing his finger at him. Next minute he had his face right up against Jacks' and their body language said a fight was about to break out. A final push in Jacks' chest and Dominic walked away. Had he seen what had happened in the corridor? I didn't put him down for standing up to anyone. He looked too weedy. Maybe I'd got him wrong. But if he'd seen what was happening, why didn't he try to stop it?

The incident with that weasel, Jacks, was replaying in my mind as I propped myself up against Will for the last dance. I needed to tell him, but not right now. I'd dealt with it in my own way. During my upbringing I'd got used to being taken advantage of – not in the same way – but in other ways. Lending money and never getting it back, making sacrifices that were never appreciated. Compromising again and again for the benefit of others in the congregation. And for what? It was one thing being selfless, as Jesus was, but quite another thing being a doormat that everyone walked all over.

Not anymore. Those days were over. I wanted to be able to fight my own battles, stand up for myself and come out on top from now on. It felt good.

In the shared taxi home I sat in the back with the girls and Dominic. Although the four of us were slim it was still quite a squeeze. Ellie insisted on having her crutches in the car instead of putting them in the boot. I think she was getting quite attached to them. She'd decorated the boring grey NHS metal and made covers for the handles. They were really quite colourful. Will was up front chatting with the driver as we made our way along the deserted coast road out of town.

Sandy and Ellie got dropped off first, then us. As we each left the taxi we all gave a portion of the fare to Dominic. It worked out well. He was a funny bugger, that Dominic. He still didn't acknowledge me even when I gave him my money. I suppose he was still pissed off that I pushed his hand away that night at the staff meal. But that was ages ago. He's got to get over it. I leaned in and gave him a peck on the cheek, as I'd done with both Sandy and Ellie and they had done to Will.

"I like your hair," he said, as I started to push the passenger door closed.

Well, that broke the ice. He even made eye contact with me but there was still no smile.

CHAPTER 6

I told Will about Jacks and his antics. He was cross that I hadn't told him at the time. Said he would have knocked his bloody head off, the jumped-up little bastard. I convinced him I'd dealt with it and there was nothing to worry about.

"But still, you should have told me," he continued. "I'm there for you, you know. How can I protect you if you don't tell me what happening?" Was I being too independent? I wasn't sure.

Monday morning. Back to work. The weekend had been fabulous – tiring but great fun. I wasn't used to these late nights but I was willing to try. The day ahead would bring the usual piles of mail to open and deliver to the appropriate person, filing left over from the end of last week, cheques to prepare for banking and, most importantly, cover notes to write as they came in. My job was all very familiar to me now and I was ready for some more challenges. I wondered if it was time to ask Mr Roades if there were any college courses he could send me on. He seemed to be pleased with the standard of my work so far, maybe he would consider investing in me.

I made tea at ten thirty, as was the routine. Mr Roades told me to close the door and take a seat when I brought his "strong with two sugars" in to him. *He must have read my mind*, I thought. I sat facing him, legs together, not crossed, as my Office Practice teacher had advised. I waited for him to hand a college prospectus to me.

"Jessica, how do you feel you're getting on at Hepworth Insurance?"

It was a straight-forward question and I felt relaxed in my answering of it. Mr Roades listened intently and nodded at the points where I slipped in some praise for the company.

"So, you value the position Hepworth has in the market and you value your position within it, is that right?"

"Yes, Mr Roades. I wouldn't want to work for any other company." I was trying to spread it on but not too thick. His face suddenly became very serious.

"Well, in that case you need to get rid of that bloody awful hair colour. If you want to keep your job here, Jessica, get your hair back to what it was or don't bother coming in tomorrow."

I was shocked. He didn't like my hair! But this was the new me, now. This is who I am.

"We have a reputation to keep, high standards to maintain, not just the managers, underwriters and loss adjusters, but everyone involved in this company. Everyone. That means YOU. Do I make myself clear?"

"Yes, Mr Roades."

I left work feeling a mixture of anger and embarrassment. The others in the office had given me some funny looks when I'd arrived that morning, no comments, just looks. I bet they knew I was in for it with the boss. But what gives him the right to tell me what hair colour I can or can't have? It's MY hair. MY decision.

Esther knew I had something on my mind that evening and told me to spit it out.

"It's not right, Esther. It's my choice, isn't it?"

"But he's the boss, darling. And so, yes, he does have the right."

"I thought I'd got away from being preached to about 'dress and grooming', constantly being told how to dress like a Christian, not to draw attention to oneself but reflect Christian attitudes in the way we present ourselves. And I'm *so* finished with all that."

"Look, there's a time and a place for everything. I'm sure you've heard that one at your meetings, haven't you?"

"King Solomon, the book of Ecclesiastes," I stated automatically. I tutted at myself as I realised my Bible education was stuck in there forever.

"So, keep your hair and your wacky clothes for the clubs and be smart at work. It's simple. We all have rules that we don't agree with in this life, but we have to knuckle down to get what we want. That's the way it is. And what's the alternative? You going to give up your job? No, I didn't think so," Esther said as I shook my head.

"So, why don't you start peeling those potatoes while I telephone my hairdresser. See if she can come round and rescue your career."

It wasn't fair. I was still seething as I took Petra for a quick walk along the beach and around the block. I'll have to buy a wig. There was no other way round it. Wear it at weekends.

The transformation took hours and left me with a shade near to my true colour, a truly uninteresting dark brown. I groaned as I looked at the result in the mirror and decided I needed a bit of a walk to clear my head. Although it was about half nine, I grabbed my jacket from the coat stand and headed east along the pebbles. I took Petra with me for safety and the white of her coat caught the moonlight as she ran a little way ahead of me. She loved the freedom and knew the area well, every little ginnel between the houses. The air was so clean and I breathed it in deeply, felt it reaching down, touching the base of my lungs.

I stood on the beach looking out to sea with Petra sitting by my side. *I'm still free*, I told myself. *I'm still me, but sometimes I've going to have to compromise for the sake of others.* That sounded a little too familiar. But this time I would feel the benefit from it. I can't give up what could be a promising career – something I never dreamed of having – for a hairstyle! After a stern word with myself I had to accept I just needed to toe the line.

I could see the glow of the Sovereign lighthouse twinkling far away and lights from a boat out on the horizon. They looked lonely, lost. Apart from that it was inky black. I turned to start making our way back and Petra chose to stay at heal.

"Off you go, girl," I encouraged her. But she stayed with me. Suddenly she stopped in her tracks and looked about her. I peered into the darkness all around trying to see what had caught her attention, but I couldn't see anything unusual. Something was irritating her, I could tell. She kept stopping and looking behind every few feet. I started to feel a little uneasy and quickened my pace.

I turned off the beach and headed down a road parked with cars both sides. The streetlights were few and far between and it wasn't that much brighter than the beach. Petra stopped again. This time she barked. Something was not right. I had that same feeling I had before when walking back from the pool. The feeling of being observed. I looked about me.

"If you've got something to say, just come out and say it," I shouted as firmly as I could into the darkness behind, trying to hide the nervousness in my voice. Silence, then I heard a shuffle, then footsteps receding. The nearest lamp was about twenty feet away and partly covered by a huge tree. It wasn't bright enough to see anything but yes, there was someone following me. I was convinced. I needed to talk to Esther.

My steps almost became a run, my heart raced, and I couldn't reach the front door soon enough. Esther was in the living room and I bounded in telling her of my suspicions. I had no idea who might be so interested in me.

"It'll just be someone else out walking their dog, Jess. Don't worry about it. Forgive me for saying it but your hair looks great." I grimaced and hung my jacket over my head.

"No! Absolutely not! That's not something I've ever been involved in and I'm certainly not going to start all that rubbish now. Dressing up like a corpse? No thank you. Anyway, don't you find it offensive?"

Will told me about the Halloween party at the end of the month. It was sure to be a great night round at his friend Harry's. Harry was known for always putting on a great party, splashing out on plenty of food, and his regular DJ always satisfied the musical tastes of his guests. It was just an excuse to get together really, just some harmless fun.

"Why should it make me feel offended, Jess?"

"Well, if you've ever lost someone close, as most people have, don't you find it funny to think that their spirits come alive and are wandering round on that particular night. And people dress up to look like them, like they've just come up out of the grave all squishy with bits missing. I think it's horrible."

"Ah, I suppose this is another one of the JW things you weren't allowed to do? So, you've never been trick or treating as a child, then? Never had fun carving out a pumpkin?"

I just smiled at Will, thinking that being given sweets by strangers, destroying perfectly good vegetables and wearing fake blood were not really things I'd ever yearned to do, Witness upbringing or not.

"Those practices about the dead and restless spirits is not what it's all about these days. It really is just about getting together and having fun, you know. So how about it? Harry's a good party thrower."

"I'm sorry Will, I just know I wouldn't enjoy something like that. I remember when I was a kid waiting for the bus home from the meeting one night. I saw a group of people dressed up shuffling along the pavement, groaning and rattling chains. There was blood dripping down their faces and dirty bandages hanging off them. It scared the life out of me, and I cried all the way home. This is one party you'll have to go to on your own, I'm afraid."

This was one event I wasn't willing to give way on. I knew I could go if I wanted to. There was no one hanging around waiting to pounce on me and tell me off for attending a pagan party, no one waiting to report me to the Elders. But I was exercising my right to choose. And for this one I chose not to go.

Will went along with Sandy, and Ellie who, by this time was walking very well unaided. Some work colleagues of Will's were there and his brother Duncan, visiting from Manchester. Of course, Will took his camera and a collapsible backdrop. He made a little money by taking everyone's photo and making up prints in his own darkroom. I got the feeling he was disappointed by my less than enthusiastic reaction when he showed me the prints. I attempted to give him some praise later on, but the moment had passed. I felt a bit mean. I could appreciate his artistry but not the gruesome subject. My evening was spent winding all the clocks back by an hour and then I had an early night. Apart from the whole demons thing I just really didn't enjoy seeing people dressed up like characters from Michael Jackson's Thriller video.

Along with many other Witnesses, 'Thriller' was an album I didn't buy. I did have suspicions, though, that some die-hard JW MJ fans would have secretly purchased it. I could picture them standing at the HMV counter at closing time, sneaking it into a carrier bag hidden between two other albums, furtively looking about to see if they've been rumbled.

The talk from the platform that Thursday night a few years ago had made me and many others get rid of almost our entire record collections. 'Should we really be listening to music, Brothers, that encourages sex before marriage, or that produces anger and hatred in us?' I recalled the speaker saying.

Kate Bush was known to include a seance in one of her videos; Michael Jackson – a professed Witness himself – was singing about rotting dead bodies rising out of graves in all their squishy glory. Was that appropriate music to listen to? Of course not. So out the records went. It was not good enough to pass them on to anyone else; they needed to be destroyed permanently with no chance of influencing anyone else. Earth, Wind and Fire; David Bowie; Queen; Culture Club; Pet Shop Boys – they all had to go and, although the act of breaking them up and ripping the covers to pieces was painful, it was the right thing to do.

My conscience was now clear. It didn't leave much in the record cabinet to get excited about. Mum's Shadows album was acceptable as Hank Marvin was a baptised Witness. But her stack of Mantovanis left me cold. And the weird but wonderful 'Snowflakes Are Dancing' by Tomita both intrigued me and hurt my ears at the same time. Our house became very quiet without music. On a Sunday evening I used to sit myself on the stool in the kitchen and listen to the Top 20. I'd slip a blank tape into the cassette recorder and, listening to the words very carefully, record the songs I felt comfortable with.

It was Friday, the end of another challenging but satisfying week at work. Esther was working a late shift at the hospital so I had the house to myself. It was my opportunity to get lost in some great music, all the stuff I'd missed out on over the years. Songs written by homosexuals, by drug-takers, by smokers and adulterers. Songs that had deliciously immoral lyrics and ones that I could lose my head in. The volume didn't matter, the higher the better - the walls of this old house were so thick who would complain anyway. Petra?

So now, as I thumbed through Esther's collection in the sideboard (and some that were clearly Will's), I felt like a kid in a sweet shop. Here were my old musical mates, Madonna, Tony Hadley, The Communards - Jimmy Somerville and Richard Coles and of course, Toyah, all back with me again. I actually, literally played the hell out of them. I considered buying a portable cassette player (a Sony Discman was too expensive) so I could listen to my favourite tunes on the way to and from work.

I was clearing up, replacing the records in their white paper sleeves then the album covers. I flopped down on the sofa, exhausted from dancing all evening. With a mug of hot chocolate in my hands I'd planned to watch the News at Ten and head off to bed. The wind had suddenly picked up making the letterbox flap and rattle furiously. A couple of times the noise had got me up out of my comfortable curled up position to open the door, expecting someone to be outside. Nope, no one there. I stuck some tape over it and that sorted it out. It wasn't stuck down so firmly that the postman wouldn't be able to just push the post through in the morning. But throughout Pevensey Bay and much of the south-east, the following day there was no postman and no post.

I watched the weather report following the news and I distinctly heard Michael Fish saying not to worry, there isn't a hurricane coming, just some strong winds.

My bed was calling so I snuggled down and considered myself lucky to be inside on a night like this. Any boats out there were in danger in winds this strong. I was half awake when Esther opened the door to my room at 2.30am.

"You awake, Jess?" she whispered.

"Yeh, what's up?"

"Can't you hear the wind? I heard something crashing outside." She moved to the window and held back the curtains. I scrambled out of bed and peered out from behind her.

"Oh my goodness!" We both looked down on the shocking scene below. The track that ran along in front of the beach houses was littered with uprooted trees, and debris from gardens. Heavy plant pots were being thrown up into the air as if made of polystyrene and bounced across the beach, smashing to pieces and their contents disappearing in the wind. One end of the old rowing boat in Esther's garden was lifting and falling with the strong gusts ready to be launched into the air. A rope was tied through the metal ring so it should be secure enough. As we took in the scene we realised there was nothing we could do. Tiles and bits of wood flew around crashing into houses, into parked cars, smashing their windows.

The sea itself sounded like a raging animal as it roared and danced about in a fury. There were no rolling waves, just torrents of water pounding the beach, the bright white froth shining in the moonlight. The sea came all the way up to the low wall in front of the house and was threatening to come over the top. There were no doors at the front otherwise it would be time to get the sandbags out. Other houses down the road were not built in the same way. Our neighbours would have a busy night ahead of them trying to protect their properties.

There were no lights on an any other houses that we could see. To the east I spotted a telegraph pole that was leaning precariously, balancing on nothing, its cables flapping and whipping about like an angry snake, severed by the violent attack of the wind. Sparks flew each time one end touched the wet ground.

"I'd better phone the council. They'll need to secure those cables before anyone gets electrocuted." Esther ran down the stairs to the phone in the hall and I followed right behind. The howling and crashing was getting louder outside and I looked about to see if there was anything I could do other than just watch the devastation. I suddenly remembered Esther's bike in the garden. I'd used it regularly and never bothered to put it back in the shed. I pulled the net curtain back from the side door and looked to see where it had ended up. It was nowhere to be seen.

Part of the fence was lying flat, its slats splayed out like fingers and the hanging baskets of winter pansies had been unhooked and were now bouncing around the garden.

Petra was whimpering in her bed. She knew there was something very wrong so I comforted her and held her tight as Esther talked to the council.

"Turn the lights on, Jess," Esther called to me. I flicked the switch but nothing happened. "No, there's no power here," she said into the receiver. "All right, yes, I will, thank you." She replaced the handset and looked worryingly at me.

"It's mayhem everywhere," she said. "The woman I just spoke to says as soon as someone can get to the cable they'll secure it, but it won't be any time soon. I'll have to report the loss of power to the electricity board as soon as I can."

"Will! Let's call Will, make sure he's all right. Thank goodness the phone still works."

He was fine, and almost moaned at us for waking him up. Over in Brighton the wind was equally fierce and with disbelief in his voice he told us of the devastation he could see from his upstairs flat. Several trees had been uprooted down both sides of the street and debris was littering the roads making it impassable. In front of the block next door the roots of a massive tree had lifted the pavement and the neighbour's wall had collapsed straight on top of a car. Fortunately, Will's block had an underground car park so his car would be all right. His voice was shaking and kept cutting out. He still had electricity for now but he could see cables flapping from the telegraph poles opposite. We knew we were all safe, assured each other we wouldn't try and go outside for any reason, just stay indoors. Promising to call again at 8am, we all went back to bed, though none of us expected to get any sleep.

The following morning Esther turned the radio on and tuned it to the local station. Reports were coming through of many cars being smashed by falling trees, buildings being torn down, bits of roofing flying about and caravan parks totally destroyed. The storm seemed to have affected mainly the south-east so presumably mum and Peter were all right being further up the country. I wondered if they were thinking of me down here.

The following few days without electricity were difficult. We had no cooker, no heating as we had storage heaters, no lighting or refrigeration. The schools and shops in the village were closed for the very same reasons and during the day people were out tidying and sweeping up the mess.

Work was extremely busy with all the claims coming in. We were a commercial insurance brokers so we didn't have to deal with the thousands of houses that were damaged, only the businesses, although that was quite enough. Five staff came down from a sister firm in Manchester to help deal with all the calls and the mountain of extra paperwork. The following days saw the postman dropping sacks and sacks of post at the door, not the usual small bundle with a rubber band around it. Each morning we had a team meeting where Mr Roades gave us all a pep talk and advised us of any new procedures. It was hard work but by the time things had begun to calm down a few weeks later, I'd learned so much about the industry. I'd shown I was capable of working under pressure and was willing to learn and adapt and it was noticed by the right person.

It was very scary to have felt and seen the power of the wind and to know that no clever man-made defences could have stopped what happened that night. It was quite a sight and made me think *this is what Armageddon will be like, no doubt*. After a worldwide war there would be some work to do to clear the place up. Of course, it would be only Jehovah's Witnesses that would be around, as they like to think, and they would all be full of smug smiles having been chosen by God to survive. Did I still believe it all? I wasn't sure, but this event certainly made me consider the fragility of life and what comes after.

I suddenly felt the reality that anyone's life could be snuffed out at any minute just like the eighteen people around the country who died during this storm. The thought made me shiver. That truth brought about a different perspective. I began to look at things in a very temporary light, knowing that my lights could go out at any moment. I resolved to make the most of every moment I'd been granted.

CHAPTER 7

Theresa called me over one day at the pool. I'd just completed my 10-mile swimming challenge for Live Aid and was walking on air. I'd done it and I was thrilled to tell her! She gave me a huge hug. "Well done, you! That's fantastic." She was really pleased but didn't know the half of what it meant to me. Now I could collect the sponsorship money and pay it into the bank.

It felt so good to be part of something that mattered. That was a feeling that I missed if I was honest. Being a Witness, knowing things about the world we live in, the planet, the future that other people, even the Governments, weren't aware of, I did feel special. That myself and all the other Witnesses on the planet could save the world. There was nothing more satisfying than that. But I wasn't so sure about it all now. With this small challenge I found myself helping out on a more local level, for the people of my own country, and with this money they would benefit sooner than they would waiting for Armageddon to arrive.

"Jess, what are you doing next Sunday? I've got my niece and nephew coming round for tea then we're going to have some fireworks in the garden. Want to join us?"

"Oh, Sunday, yeah, what time?"

"Make your way over about three-ish while it's still light, then we'll eat about five."

"Sounds good. I don't suppose Neil would be able to drive me back, would he?"

"I'm sure he wouldn't mind, no problem."

Since my suspicions had grown about someone following me, I didn't want to take any chances. Maybe I was being paranoid, but I couldn't shake the feeling that I was being watched. One afternoon, when I'd got home from work and the house was empty, I sat down and really had a good think about it. Was there some random pervert hanging around in Pevensey who got a kick out of making people feel scared? I couldn't work it out and tried again to put it to the back of my mind.

Guy Fawkes Night. Another worldly celebration not mentioned in the Bible. Wedding anniversaries were not mentioned either but the Witnesses still celebrated those, for some reason. Now I would be able to see the fireworks from close up, not just peering out of my bedroom window hoping to catch a glimpse of the neighbours' efforts.

The evening at Theresa and Neil's was just lovely. Theresa's niece and nephew, Charlotte and Spencer, were lively kids and very friendly and they adored their aunty. Tea was finger food which we took out into the garden and sat around throwing rubbish onto the fire in the metal dustbin. Spencer looked up from the picture of a dumper truck he was colouring in.

"Mummy's having a meltdown," announced the four-year-old out of nowhere. He continued his artwork.

"Oh, right, well, maybe a night on her own will do her good then." I couldn't think what else to say to such a comment.

"Yeh, Annabel's not coping well with being a single mum," Theresa explained. "She needs a proper break from the kids. Terry has them every other weekend and he's really good with them but she's a delicate soul. Has awful depressive moods at times. I've had to take the kids to school several days recently. She can't get herself up some mornings. I'm very worried about her."

"Doesn't sound good, sorry to hear that. My mum suffers with depression, has done for years. She takes medication but that only seems to take the edge off. It's not a cure, unfortunately. Maybe swimming would do her good?" Discussing mental health issues made me realise I hadn't talked to mum for a while. I'd better call her tomorrow afternoon after the meeting.

Bang!!! There was Neil letting off the first of the fireworks without telling us. We all just refilled our plates and dashed out to the garden, heads held high looking up into the night sky. It was truly wonderful! Magical! A little bit scary, though, watching Neil light the things at arm's length and jumping back before they launched themselves. Some of them shot straight up before exploding into a shower of sparkles raining down before disappearing into nothing. Others whirled in a spiral making a whizzing sound till they burned themselves out.

Charlotte and Spencer giggled and gasped as they craned their necks following the line of travel higher and higher into the dark sky. Some shattered quickly and fizzled out disappointingly. Others tumbled like a rainbow-coloured waterfall or floated and merged with the one that came next. And there were sparklers that we held in our fingers. I was quite wary at first, thinking the stick would surely burn me. It was great, and I knew I was giggling like a child. Neil commented that I was behaving as if I'd never seen a firework before.

Theresa had made toffee apples and there were jam doughnuts too. The sticky sweetness clung to my fingers even after I'd licked them. The fireworks were over far too quickly. I could have watched them all night. We ended the evening each huddled in a blanket around the roaring fire, kids asleep – one on my lap, the other on Theresa's. We talked about all kinds of things, life and love and family – although I didn't go into detail about mine too much. I didn't want to spoil the atmosphere. It had been a lovely, family evening and I left feeling I'd made some new friends.

Being with those gorgeous children made me think of my own little niece Bethany, though. She was no doubt growing up fast and I'd only seen her once. I wondered: if I rang Peter and just asked him nicely, he might agree to me spending some time with her? How could I possibly be a bad influence on a toddler? He made me feel like a criminal. Peter was overreacting and being very selfish. What would his daughter think of him in years to come when Bethany discovers that she has an aunty? That he was the one who has kept us apart? How's he going to explain that one to her? But miracles do happen as they say. If it ends up only taking a phone call, then it's got to be worth a try. I needed to plan the call and tread carefully in what I said, how I worded things. It wouldn't do to have the wrong tone of voice and sound accusatory, much as I wanted to blast out my feelings about the whole thing. No, I needed to think. I needed to go for a long walk.

I loved walking. When we lived in Eastbourne before moving north we'd done lots of walking as kids; myself, Peter and mum, with Kathy and Greg and their eight children. Country walks, scrumping apples or plums along the way. We tramped through fields, over streams, for miles, kids crying and moaning for drinks or food, and all of us feeling so exhausted on the way back we had to count the lampposts just to keep going.

It was a bright, crisp, autumn morning and I felt like I could do with a proper walk, not just to the Aqua Bar and back but far enough that my legs would get a good workout. Peelings Lane, a track that connected Stone Cross with Pevensey, was one of our starting points years ago and so that's where I thought I'd head. I packed my rucksack with a bottle of water, crisps and a banana, plasters in case my trainers rubbed and my Bella magazine to sit and read before heading back. I was well wrapped up against the cold with my purple gloves, crocheted scarf and bobble hat. Esther was kind enough to give me a lift to the top of Friday Street as she was going to the market in Hailsham, and I set out on my walk with the sun in my face and the traffic behind me.

The light fell through onto the track as the trees partially blocked the sun's beams, and moving shapes appeared ahead of my feet, dancing and swirling as the breeze made the sparce leaves shiver. The smell was one of dampness, of woody earth, decay, like the bottom of a hamster cage. There had been many creatures at Kathy's over the years; dogs, cats, rabbits, birds, chickens, snakes, frogs and a stuffed badger being among them, all lovingly cared for and part of the family. But, strangely, I never remember there being any hamsters.

Theirs had been a happy home, or so it appeared. That's why Peter and I spent so much time there and why it was the first place I thought to go when Ray and I needed to move on from the campsite. That seemed so long ago but really it had only been three years.

Lost in my thoughts, the sounds and fragrances of the woodland all around me, I wondered what all the kids were all doing now. Nerys, one of the twins around my age was who I got on with best. She'd got married last year, pushed into it, I thought, with the fear of being disfellowshipped hanging over her head if she and her fiancé happened to end up in the sack. Not a good reason to get married, surely, but they weren't the only ones who tied the knot in a hurry. I'd heard of so many young marriages amongst Witnesses. It was a way of staying safe, of not being put out of the congregation – get married quickly, then you're free to have all the sex you want! I wondered if many of those marriages had lasted beyond the first year.

My walk took me past a derelict house. It was down an overgrown lane behind a row of ramshackle buildings, all having stood there, in that condition, for many years. As kids we'd made a detour off the main track, sneaking into its terrifying emptiness. In our plimsolls we tip-toed across the broken floorboards, jumping across the gaps. We opened squeaky cupboards in what was left of the kitchen, and froze, listening out for footsteps coming to shoo us away. Shattered glass lay on the abandoned, rotting rug by the fireplace, a pile of unused wood in the corner. Beetles skittered across the floors as we moved planks of wood to get to the staircase. We dared each other to climb them, to jump over the gaping holes. *Tell us what's up there. Perhaps there's a dead body lying on the bed!* A door creaked and we ran, scarpered out of that place as fast as we could, the toddlers being dragged behind. And there the house still stood. As spooky as before, with a few more smashed windows and the outer walls being overrun with suffocating ivy.

Further along, three new houses had been built. Their smart gardens looked as if they'd just been planted, short stubby bushes with space to grow lined the front path to the door. Winter pansies held their faces up to the sun and small evergreen bushes shivered in the breeze. What a beautiful place to live. Secluded and peaceful, surrounded by woodland.

The walk was doing me good, I could feel it. I had space to lay out my thoughts, to go back over the events of the past weeks and months. To think about mum, about Will, where my life was going. I'd heard it said so many times, as people dropped off from attending meetings, that they'll never be happy. No, they'll always feel as if there was something missing in their lives. Was there something missing in my life? No, I didn't think so. I had a steady job, a wonderful boyfriend, a secure home and I was building a solid network of friends. I also had hobbies and interests – swimming, music and fashion. I was in danger of being a normal person.

But I no longer had important people in my life – my dad and my sisters, and mum and Peter, and my old friends. So, perhaps there was something missing. But somehow, I wasn't taking the blame for that any longer. It was their choice if some of them had rejected me because I didn't wish to be a Witness anymore. And it was the choice of others if they had chosen the religion's rules over me, their daughter, sister, friend. But I was still here, still alive and on this planet, they could get in touch with me if they wanted. I suppose many thought they were doing the right thing. But nothing would make me turn around and go back to that suffocating organisation, nothing. Not even to be with my family again. It just wouldn't work and I knew it would make me miserable.

Up ahead I could see some movement in amongst the trees. The colours stood out against the greenery – the purple of the woman's skirt, the pink of her thick slouchy cardigan, a scarf thrown around her neck. On her arm she held a wicker basket. A red setter scampered around her feet then darted over to the man as he called him.

"Pebbles! Sit."

The man and the dog stayed back as the woman reached into the bushes and then placed something in her basket. Horse chestnuts. Conkers. As I got nearer to the couple I almost didn't want to disturb them, just walk past, but something about them was familiar.

"Hello Jessica, how are we? Kathy, over here!" he called, "it's Jessica. What are you doing here?" Greg nudged the dog and he bounded over towards me, sniffing my hand as I held it out to him. He nuzzled his head against my leg. Pebbles remembered me.

"Greg, Kathy. Fancy seeing you here. Just come for a walk, didn't expect to bump into you."

Kathy stepped out from the leaves, several clinging onto her skirts. She brushed herself down.

"Jess, oh my! Why haven't you been round to see us?"

This was Kathy all over. Straight to the point, no messing around.

"Your mum said you'd moved down here so we expected to see you. She said you're living in Pevensey Bay."

"Yes, I do. It's lovely out there. I go for a swim most mornings." Although these two had been my friends, almost second parents, I still didn't feel like getting into conversations too personal with them. They had seen me at my most vulnerable and, yes, I was still embarrassed about the whole thing. But also, I'd moved on. I wasn't a part of their religion, and therefore their lives any longer, and I knew they would keep me at arms' length because of it. It would be foolish of me to try to be good friends with them again.

We walked along the path for a while in gentle conversation. Kathy updated me on what the kids were doing. The youngest was now in secondary school, Greg still had his job at the Post Office in town. Kathy was pioneering this month now that all the kids were back at school. They both seemed happy enough. Pebbles wanted to walk next to me. He kept sniffing my clothes, perhaps he could smell Petra. Our journey took us further towards Pevensey and the breaks in the woodland allowed the sunlight to warm our faces just a tiny bit. At one time there would have been a cuppa in a teashop and a circuit around the Pevensey castle but not any longer.

"That's far enough for me, love." Kathy called to Greg. "Arthritis setting in, Jess. At least you won't have the privilege of getting old."

There she goes. She can't help herself. Mum had been saying for years that Armageddon was coming very soon; that it would be here before I started secondary school. But I went through my five years there, no sign of it happening. Then it was, "oh, you won't get married in this system, Armageddon's just around the corner." I was old enough to get married now. I guess they would now be saying it'll be here before I have children. And Kathy is so convinced that the end of this world system will happen before I get old – well – if it keeps her focussed and gives her strength, who am I to knock it? It's just that this same old chestnut had been spouted for so many years, and nothing had changed, the world had just got worse, with no sign of God stepping in. There were couples I know that decided not to bring children into this world, to wait till the paradise is here before they start a family. Now they are elderly, not able to produce kids, and where is Armageddon? And I wonder how those childless couples feel now.

"Want to come back for a cup of coffee? I think Pebbles would like you to."

Although the invitation surprised me somewhat I took them up on the offer. I had to admit to feeling a little on edge, fearing how the conversation might go, but this was Kathy and Greg, my friends. I had missed them and I wanted to spend some time with them. Just this once.

Greg still had his old Rover and it took just a few minutes in the car to get to their house. They used to have two houses knocked into one. That was to accommodate all their children. A couple of years ago they reverted back to just number four as the older kids had moved out.

Greg's mum, Joan, still lived with them, and her commode was still in the corner. She sat with a blanket over her knees, lost in her own thoughts, and didn't appear to recognise me when I said hello.

The coffee was good. The homebaked flapjack made with heavy dark sugar was delicious. The fire wasn't lit but we sat in front of it as if it was glowing. On the coffee table were two magazines, the latest editions of the Watchtower and Awake. Both now in full colour. On the shelf underneath was a pile of the same, ready to distribute to all of Kathy's Route Calls - people who had shown an interest and who had the mags every fortnight. She was good at talking to people and no doubt conducted several Bible studies throughout the week.

"So, how's everyone in the congregation? I've bumped into the Peacocks a few times in Pevensey."

"Yes, they moved out there recently. Ginny is my pioneer partner, in fact. We work together three times a week. Oh, I think everyone's all right. Ticking along, you know. Hard times come along and you kind of see people struggling to get to meetings and looking a bit down. But they get through it; with Jehovah's help, they get over their troubles and move on."

There was always a lesson in whatever Kathy said, or at least, that's how it felt. That she was trying to teach me something, a life lesson. I tried to keep the conversation light-hearted, telling her about my new job, how much I loved it. That I'd met some lovely, normal people since I'd been down here. My swimming and my goal of one day doing a lifeguard's course.

I'd finished my coffee and poured another one from the pot. There was a jug of milk on the tray and it was still warm. One small square of flapjack remained on the plate and Kathy saw me eyeing it. With a nod she indicated that I could take it.

She listened in silence. I couldn't tell if she was happy for me or not; she never gave much away. One of the cats had climbed on her lap and she was engrossed in fussing it, stroking and flattening its fluffy fur from head to tail. Greg was off doing something, somewhere in the house or garden – no one really knew what Greg got up to.

"We have a special speaker on Sunday, do you fancy coming along?"

Oh, for goodness sake, Kathy. Give it a rest!

I had to answer her, and honestly, but part of me just wanted to get up and leave.

I huffed. "To be truthful, Kathy, no. I don't want to go."

And then she asked me a question that opened up a conversation that lasted well into the evening, with revelations I hadn't expected. She simply said: "Why?" She then sat back, still stroking the cat, and let me answer it.

Here was my chance to explain my feelings about all that had gone on, but I didn't know where to start. I just came out with the first thing that came to mind.

"Because I don't think it is the true religion and it's full of hypocrites. There are just as many liars and deceivers and bullies in the Truth as there are out of it, and I feel like I've been conned all my life. There are power hungry Elders who make things up as they go along, ruining people's lives, causing people to kill themselves. Is that enough reason? Or shall I go on?"

She stayed silent. So I went on.

"And the blood issue. I don't agree with the instruction not to have blood transfusions, allowing children to die when they could be saved. I thought we were supposed to view life as precious. It's wrong, Kathy. And this disfellowshipping rule is completely unbalanced, too. It splits up families. Grandchildren grow up not knowing their own grandparents, aunts, uncles, cousins. It's cruel and I'm sure God doesn't approve."

I was getting angry, my voice turning into a whine, so I stopped. I slurped some more coffee.

"Well, that's a lot of reasons not to come to the meeting! Are you accurate in all that you've just stated, though, Jess? You said that the religion is 'full of hypocrites', is that really true? Am I a hypocrite?

She didn't allow me to answer but carried on.

"You say you feel as though you've been conned. And that there are liars in the Truth. What do they lie about, then?"

This one I *did* want to answer.

"The number of times I've heard it from the platform that all those who have rejected Jehovah are thieves, adulterers, criminals, liars, murderers – it's just not true Kathy. Think about people you know, perhaps relatives, who are not Witnesses. Are they bad people? Are they vicious drunkards, drug-takers, in league with the devil, dishonest, violent towards their children? No. Well, maybe some of them are, of course, but the Elders can't just make sweeping statements like that. They seem happy to put people in boxes, tar them all with the same brush and discard them if they're not Witnesses. These people just don't want the magazines that you offer at the door, it's as simple as that.

She took her eyes away from the cat for a moment and looked at me. Joan shuffled in her seat, and had clearly and silently released a foul smell. Greg took after her in that way, perhaps that's why he always went off to do his own thing.

Wafting my hand, I gave her more detail about the people who had come into my life recently, Esther, Will, Theresa, Sandy, Ellie (I left out the part about their sexuality as I wanted to stay on the subject and, it wasn't important). I explained how thoughtful they were, considerate and patient. And how accepting. There was no air of judgement about them, none of them looked down their noses at me.

"Jehovah's Witnesses think they are the only group of people who have God's favour. The only group that will survive Armageddon and everyone else will be killed. That can't be right, can it? They think they are special. But they're not."

Kathy took a deep breath and started to answer me. And I thought I knew exactly what she would say. She would come out with the stock answers: we are all imperfect, even the Elders, we all try to do our best but we get it wrong sometimes. And I knew the scripture she would quote to me: Colossians chapter 3 verse 13, "Keep putting up with one another and forgiving one another freely…". There was really no point talking about this, there would be no way forward.

"You know, Jess…" She stumbled. I could see her trying to gather her thoughts and arrange the words before releasing them. "Yes, there are things wrong with the Organisation, and you're right, some of the rules are questionable, I have to agree with you on those things. But…. but…."

Her agreeing with me was an eye opener, somewhat. This was Kathy, who'd been a baptised Jehovah's Witness for many years, a pioneer, a faithful wife and a good mother. A woman who put the Truth first in her life, raised her children in the faith, sometimes at cost to herself. I'd expected her to defend the Organisation wholeheartedly, and I wondered if she had confessed her doubts to anyone else or kept them private. It was never acceptable to question the Elders or their decisions, their instructions. The word 'apostate' was thrown around at the slightest inkling that someone was having doubts and the label quickly spread around the congregation. Once that label was attached it could never be removed and the 'apostate' was avoided like the plague.

She shook her head as if ridding herself of the subject, now it had been raised. She obviously didn't want to go there, didn't wish to elaborate, perhaps she feared being disloyal, even if only to me.

"Let's talk about that another time, yes? Listen, Jess, there's something important I need to tell you."

At this point she reached over and took my hand in hers and moved herself to the edge of her seat. I looked in her eyes, a frown formed on her brow, and I suddenly felt afraid of what she was about to say. I didn't have any idea what it might be, but it warranted silence and my full attention. What she proceeded to tell me shook me to the core like nothing I'd ever experienced.

CHAPTER 8

Kathy continued: "When you came down here with Ray, he stayed on after you left, as you know. Greg had a regular Bible study with him and he made great progress. He came to all the meetings, assemblies, answered up during the Watchtower discussion every Sunday. He even did the Bible reading a few times at the Thursday night meeting."

I grimaced at the thought of Ray; tall, lanky Ray in a suit. No, it wouldn't have been his natural look. I'd only ever seen him in casual clothes.

"Then he made even more progress when he pioneered, eventually being invited to work at Bethel in the printing department. He was doing so well."

I didn't like where this was going. Had he suddenly realised he'd got himself mixed up with a cult? Was he blaming me for introducing him to these religious nutters?

I hadn't heard that much about Ray after I left him down here, just that he was studying, so this was all news to me. My! He'd really gone for it all. Got caught up their sticky web. At the same time, for me he was the furthest thing from my mind as I had to concentrate on my own life and position within the Truth. It was strange hearing his name spoken, imagining him accepting the Truth. 'Brother Ray.' It sounded so weird.

"He moved on from the Beefeater very soon after you left. He got a full-time job at Bill Burton's carpet shop, as well as some evening bar work at a restaurant in town I think, and then he moved out into a flat of his own. Got baptised at the District assembly two years ago. Do you remember his younger brother, Dane?"

Yes, I did remember Dane. A very different character to Ray. When I had left home and travelled back to the campsite to stay with Ray, Dane was there as well. A smoker and a joker, he made it quite clear I was not welcome, that I'd messed up their plans to work and travel across the country. I suppose I did spoil things for them, turning up unannounced and eventually taking Ray in a completely different direction. When the two of us got the coach down to Eastbourne Dane was left to pack up the tent and make his way back home to Oldham.

"Well, he came down from Oldham to visit Ray and stayed about a week. They came round for a meal once or twice. Dane seemed very different to Ray, a bit of a wild one, I thought, but, nice enough I suppose."

Her hand still holding mine, I didn't know where this was going and wished she'd just hurry up. The cat tried to jump up onto my lap but I pushed her off. I didn't want any distractions.

Her voice changed. She softly spoke the words that told me what this was all about and the single sentence was enough.

"Dane brought his motorbike down."

I immediately put my hand up.

"Stop!"

I now knew what was coming. I swallowed, not wanting to have it confirmed.

"Oh no, Kathy. Don't say it."

I took a minute to steel myself for the full revelation and asked the question:

"How bad was it? Just tell me that."

"As bad as it could get, Jess. They got him to hospital straight away and started setting him up with some matched blood but then....one of the nurses found a card in his wallet."

It was something he'd written out himself stating that under no circumstances should he be given a blood transfusion as he was a Jehovah's Witness. He would accept minor blood fractions and hemodilution but not whole blood. They had to take it seriously as it had been signed and witnessed by two people - Elders as it happened.

"No, Kathy, no!!"

Her hand tightened on mine.

"He passed away never having regained consciousness. He would have known no pain, at least."

She allowed me some time to absorb it all. I was too shocked to cry. I rubbed my temples in the hope the information would untangle itself in my head, that I could get it straight.

I needed to vocalise this. "So, he'd made up a card to say he didn't want a blood transfusion because he was a Witness?" I'd heard of other Witnesses having done that. It was a safeguard against being transfused against their will, if they were unable to communicate in any way. He took it seriously, obviously.

"Yes, they found out that he had also got it put on his medical records, so there was no doubt what his wishes were."

"Ray, you bloody fool!" I shouted, scaring the cat away. I needed some air and opened the window. "So presumably if he'd had blood he might still be alive now?"

"That's what we never got to find out. The doctors would only talk to his parents, naturally."

"But the fact that he was carrying a *card*. That he'd made up his mind so completely…."

Kathy was speaking in the past tense, but I suddenly realised I didn't know when this had taken place.

"When exactly did this happen, Kathy?"

She looked embarrassed as she revealed it was just after I'd moved down to Pevensey Bay. Over a year ago! A memorial service was held for him at the Kingdom Hall and his parents came and took his body back home for cremation.

"So, hang on a minute. I was here when all this happened?" I huffed my annoyance. "Why didn't anyone tell me? Did mum know?"

Kathy and mum were very good friends and spoke on the phone often. There was no doubt in my mind that mum would have heard about this. Why didn't she tell me? Why didn't *someone* tell me? Surely, I had a right to know? But I knew mum was good at keeping secrets, as she'd done with Bethany's birth.

"It was a difficult time for you, we all realised that, what with you getting back on your feet again after being reinstated, and then moving away from home. We talked about whether you should be told or not and came to the conclusion that it would be best for you if we kept it quiet. We didn't even tell his old workmates at the Beefeater, knowing that you'd got your old job back. Clearly, they still haven't heard otherwise they would have mentioned it."

"I can't believe it." That was all I could say. There was too much to take in. I busied myself by making a cup of tea for us both. As I stood waiting for the kettle to boil through the kitchen window I observed yet another cat eyeing up the chickens in their enclosure. It sat watching, ready to pounce, dents in the chicken wire where previous attempts had failed. The chucks couldn't escape the cat's penetrating stares and its relentless pacing up and down, looking for a way in. Such patience. It would get them in the end.

I brought the teapot and cups in on the tray, my hand shaking as I added the milk. Kathy indicated not to bother making one for Joan.

"Please believe me, we did the right thing, Jess. If you'd have known about it at the time it would have really knocked you for six. We were all so sure you would start back at the meetings straight away down here, you know, now you had a fresh start. But as time went on and you hadn't shown your face it just got left. I knew you'd turn up one day so – today's the day, I suppose."

Joan still sat looking out of the window. It seemed she didn't do much else these days. We drank our tea in silence. A few tears escaped from my eyes, maybe Kathy had shed all of hers when it happened.

Part of me wanted to stay and talk, part of me wanted to go, to walk, to think, undisturbed. I chose the latter even though it was getting late. Kathy understood. We hugged. She told me not to be a stranger, which I found a little odd. She knew, or presumed, I was having a relationship with Will, that I was a practicing fornicator, as the Organisation would have it, and yet she still wanted me to keep in touch. This was confusing to say the least, and that *did* in fact make her a hypocrite. I decided to put that issue to one side for now and consider all that I'd just been told.

CHAPTER 9

My walk home was very long. It was dark, but not too late and my fears about being followed were pushed aside as I made my way home. I had more serious things to think about. As I passed the Beefeater on my right, I considered popping in to say hi to everyone but wasn't really in the right frame of mind. Long straight roads took me to Marsden Road where I headed into the estate and took a shortcut past Bishop Bell school through to Pevensey Bay Road. My feet knew where to go: straight to the beach, and the remainder of the walk home was along the pebbled shore, sparcely lit by a few lampposts. I stopped a few times to breathe in the winter air, feeling numb to everything around me, and to go over the facts about the ending of Ray's life.

All that he'd learned about the paradise, about death in this system must have really gone deep into his heart, that was clear. That if anyone faithful lost their life before Armageddon then they would remain in God's memory and be resurrected when the survivors have brought the earth back to the condition it should be. Death held no fear for Ray. He'd rather die than be unfaithful by having blood. Was that faith? Or was it obedience to the Organisation? He must have been so sure that what he'd been taught was the absolute truth, to be prepared to sacrifice his life like that. Must have trusted the seven members of the Governing Body in New York wholeheartedly.

I recalled that only a few years ago in 1982, a change in thinking had occurred. It was spelled out in the Watchtower that, as blood had become better understood by scientists, we were now allowed to accept a process called haemodilution. This was a process in which, immediately before surgery, a portion of a patient's own blood is removed and replaced with a volume expander. Or, to be more precise, it was no longer a disfellowshipping offence, as was taking whole blood. The Governing Body explained that there were parts of blood that the body could not live without and other bits that it could regenerate all by itself. At that point, with Jehovah's direction, of course, it was decided that although red cells, white cells, platelets and plasma were unacceptable, it now became a matter of a Christian's own conscience to accept haemodilution. On his card, Ray had said he was ok with that. Oh Ray! You poor thing!

I reached home and once through the front door, toed off my trainers and climbed the stairs. I just wanted to lie down, in silence, in the dark. I didn't hear Esther arriving home, or Will turning up later with fish and chips. I couldn't eat any of it. Once I'd explained the events of the day, they understood but it sparked a conversation about the blood issue. As Will sat on the edge of my bed and Esther at the dressing table I could see them struggling to grasp the depth of Ray's faith, his absolute belief in the resurrection. The pained looks on their faces, and frowns of incredulity showed the difference between us. They were free of the indoctrination I'd been subjected to all my life. They were adults and could choose what they believed in, or not. Was the resurrection something I still accepted? The belief had been one of my strongest – there was no doubt in my mind that my ancestors would be alive again, back here on earth. I would greet and get to know my fifty times great grandmother; William Shakespeare; Mary Queen of Scots; Elvis! And I had no fear about dying, myself, believing that as soon as I snuffed it, I'd wake up again with all my loved ones around me ready to welcome me back. I was so certain.

But now, my conviction had weakened. My trust in the Organisation had been shaken after having received their harsh treatment and since then everything they'd ever taught me had come into question.

Esther and Will respected my wishes to be left alone for a while and went downstairs, Esther gently draping an extra blanket on me and closing the door.

During the rest of the evening and the following days I dug deep in my memory. I tried to recall the scriptures that spoke of the dead coming back to life, loved ones breathing again, in perfect health. What if I could let go of the past and recapture that certainty again? To be rock solid in my beliefs as I once was. What if I'd got it all wrong, that the Witnesses were in fact the only true religion as they claimed? The only group of Christians on earth with God's favour? What if it was all true?

My heart had a heavy ache and a sadness bore down upon my shoulders. Work was difficult to concentrate on, my colleagues noticed and commented on the change in my demeanour. I just said I'd had some bad news and thankfully they didn't ask questions. They made me tea - cup after cup, all day, bless them. Sandy invited me round, said they were there for me if I needed a chat. But how could I explain everything to them? Where would I even start? I felt so alone with all my thoughts running this way and that, felt there was really no one who could possibly understand the way my mind was working, being pulled in both directions at once. It was exhausting.

My sadness continued. I rang mum and had a go at her for not telling me about Ray. Her tone was unapologetic and she stated that it was for my own good and that was that. No further discussion was necessary. She'd been shocked at the time, so was Peter, although he'd never met Ray. The news of a young life snuffed out in such a violent manner was devastating for anyone to hear.

I hated feeling so down and wanted to get myself out of this pit of despair. In the past, on hearing of the death of someone, it was easier to deal with. Their death was temporary, they'd be back soon enough. We just had to keep ourselves busy for the remainder of this wicked system until Armageddon came and God sorted everything out. Now I didn't have that to fall back on. Now I had a million doubts – where exactly was Ray right now? Was his soul a separate being, after all, that was at this moment up in heaven with God and Jesus Christ? Was he in Hell? Purgatory? Was he simply in a deep sleep? Would he come back as a spirit and play tricks on us all? Would his family and friends really be able to see him again? Did his parents and his brother need to become Witnesses now then, if they're the only ones who will survive Armageddon?

My head was spinning with the intensity of these thoughts and, try as I did, I just couldn't shake them. They were there with me from the moment I woke up to the moment I fell asleep, while I ate, while I worked, while I washed the dishes. I needed some help to clarify things. I needed to hear from the horse's mouth, once again, what exactly is the condition of the dead.

I needed to hear about the paradise; how the animals would be at peace with one another, the lamb playing with the wolf, the mouth of the lion being shut. Nations not lifting up sword with other nations, the sword becoming a ploughshare, no greed, no violence, no pain. How there will be an abundance of food for everyone and all of man's desires would be satisfied.

I longed for these uplifting words. I ached for the comfort that only a spiritual voice could provide.

I needed to get back to the meetings.

"Have you lost your mind?!! What on earth are you thinking, Jess?" Will was shouting at me.

"You don't understand, you can't possibly understand. This is something I need to do, I need the encouragement from the meetings, I need to settle things in my mind."

Will was exasperated as he tried to get me to think back, to remember how badly I had suffered at the hands of this Organisation. How their treatment of me, and others like me, had affected my mental and physical health.

"They almost destroyed you! Remember Alan. Don't forget what they've done to so many people, with their heartless cruel rules, Jess. How could you even contemplate going back to them? I don't get it."

I overheard a conversation in the kitchen between Will and Esther the following Friday night. Not that I'm an eavesdropper, I just happened to be outside the kitchen and Will's voice, in particular, was quite unrestrained.

"It just doesn't make sense, mum," he whined. "I mean, the effort Jess has gone to to free herself of their suffocating hold on her. Her family have openly rejected her, her friends have abandoned her, and now she wants to go back!"

"It happens to a lot of people when they lose someone, Will. I remember when my father died, I didn't know what to do with my feelings. I had so many questions and no one to answer them. I went to three different churches hoping to get some comfort at least but I just came away with even more questions."

"She'll set herself back, I just know it. They'll wrap themselves around her and then ditch her again for some reason. It won't last."

He was clattering around with saucepans and cutlery, banging things on the top in his anger.

"But you've just got to let her do it. It's her life."

"Yes, but who'll be picking up the pieces when she gets let down again, mum? I love Jess, and she knows I'd support her with anything she wanted to do but she's making a huge mistake with this one." I heard him release a sigh that seemed to come up from his boots.

"I can't stop her, can I?"

One crisp Sunday afternoon Will walked with me up to the harbour and we had a drink in one of the restaurants there. It was busy with locals having their Sunday lunch but we managed to get a couple of stools at the bar. I had a warming brandy and held it in my cupped hands to raise its temperature. I knew there was something on Will's mind. He'd been quite for the whole of the walk there.

"Spit it out, Will. What's up?"

He chuckled. "How do you know me so well? It's just a suggestion, see what you think."

I was keen to hear what he was going to say but I suddenly felt a tap on my shoulder.

"Jessica!"

"Ginny, Geoff." I could really have done without those two right at that moment.

"You look well, Jess. Have you changed your hair or something?"

"Yes, that was a while ago now. You OK?"

"Oh, yes, we're all right," she said in her sing song manner. "The public talk was very good this morning, I wish you'd been there. The title was 'Returning to Jehovah', you'd have enjoyed it."

I didn't respond.

"Hello, Will, nice to meet you. Well, we'd best be getting along. Be nice to see you at a meeting sometime Jess. Time's getting on, you know. And what with that storm.... Well, you'll remember what Jesus said about natural disasters being a sign that we're in the Last Days of this system? Have a think about it, Jess. Anyway, nice to see you. Bye for now."

And off they went.

"She's got that wrong. A typical JW, ever so slightly bending the scriptures to meet their own purposes. What Jesus actually said was that there would be earthquakes in one place after another, not a random hurricane on the south coast of England."

"She's so keen to get you back to the meetings. Intense," Will remarked as we watched them leave through the double doors.

I couldn't comment. I couldn't reassure Will that Ginny was wasting her time, that they'd never catch me in a Kingdom Hall ever again. I wasn't able to promise that.

"What were you going to say, Will, before we were rudely interrupted?"

"I think you should try out some other faiths, see what other people believe. You don't know what's out there. If it's comfort you want why not look into Buddhism? They're all about peace and tranquillity. You might just find what you're looking for somewhere other than the JWs."

I knew in my heart there was no way I'd take Will up on his suggestion. Every other religion was false, based on traditions and involved rituals and icons. That's what I'd been taught anyway. But I really didn't want to burst Will's bubble. He'd been good enough to give some consideration to how I was feeling, what was going through my mind and I loved him for it.

"We'll see," was all I could promise him.

It was far too cold to swim in the sea at the moment so I threw myself into pool lengths every day after work. I went at it with strength and determination to see if I could get these feelings out of my system. By the end of each week I was actually, literally exhausted and went to bed unusually early on Friday and Saturday nights. I didn't feel much like going out to Dixieland or even round to Sandy and Ellie's place. Just wanted to be in my own space for a while in the hope of working things out.

Peter rang me unexpectedly one Tuesday night. It was quite late, but then I remembered he would have just finished the Tuesday Book Study. I'd phoned mum a couple of weeks ago and she'd sounded a bit cagey I thought, and Peter now gave me news that surprised the life out of me.

I remembered Charlie from my old congregation. He was a happy sort of fella, helpful and kind-hearted and he'd been round to the house on a couple of occasions when the meeting for field service was held at mum's years ago. So now, Peter told me, he and mum had hooked up! Well, I never! It was quite a shock to hear, since I'd never known mum to have any male interests since dad left in '75.

I presumed she'd be on her own for the rest of her life. As long as Charlie could cope with mum's mood swings and occasional stubbornness they could actually have a good life together. One thing was for sure, it wouldn't be a long engagement. They never were in the Truth, no matter what ages the couple was. Although it was a surprise, this was actually very good news and I felt pleased for her. She might even mellow towards me if she's happier in herself, who knows?

During the phone call Peter didn't ask how I was, or what I was doing. I was desperate to ask after Bethany and wondered if I should take the opportunity to ask if I could spend some time with her. But his tone was short, as short as the conversation, and before I knew it he'd hung up. Perhaps it would be better if I wrote a letter.

Kathy would be excited to hear mum's news. Her attempt years ago to pair mum off with Greg's younger brother Larry had fallen at the first hurdle. They hadn't even gone on a date. I could tell her face to face if I went along to the meeting on Sunday. Yes, that's what I'll do. It wouldn't be easy, sitting inside a Kingdom Hall again, but it's where I needed to be. That's where God's spirit is after all and more than anything else right now I could do with a portion of it.

CHAPTER 10

Of course, I had to wear a skirt. Trousers were still not acceptable for women. But the only skirt I now owned didn't even cover my knees. I had to risk the disapproving looks, and they started as I walked from the bus stop towards the Hall. Ginny, of all people, was the first one that spotted me as she drove by. Her simultaneous frantic wave and right turn into the car park almost resulted in a collision. Silly woman.

"Jess! How lovely to see you! I knew you'd find your way back here eventually." She got out of the car after hurriedly parking and looked me up and down. I knew she'd clocked my skirt length in that moment. "Your boyfriend didn't fancy coming along then?"

"Not today, Ginny."

Linking her arm through mine and leading me into the Hall, she tried to get me to take a seat next to her and Geoff, but I peeled away from her grip and made my way to the ladies instead. This meeting was on my terms, I would sit where I wanted. At that first meeting back, Kathy was pleasantly surprised to see me sitting in the middle row and she and Greg chose seats nearby. Her wink said, 'well done.' She didn't need to smother me with hugs and kisses. Having some exciting news to tell Kathy took my mind off the significance of being back inside a Kingdom Hall and I was desperate to tell her about mum. However, as usual, Kathy was busy floating around the Hall speaking to people, handing in her Not Home sheet to the Book Study conductor, and collecting more magazines and books from the literature counter. She was a busy little Witness. And Greg was off doing whatever it is that Greg did. So I sat in my seat and got my Bible out in preparation for the meeting to start.

It felt very strange being inside a Kingdom Hall again, especially as I'd sworn that I'd never set foot in one ever again. I'd left my last meeting in a terrible rage and with sore knuckles. That seemed so long ago now. But things change. I had changed. Ray's death had woken me up spiritually and now I had to give it all another chance.

The Hall hadn't changed. It still had that institutional smell. The same dusky pink curtains and battle grey hard-wearing carpet tiles. New seats, though, much more comfortable than the plastic ones from a few years ago. The noise of the train running on the line directly behind the Hall was still a huge distraction and the speakers stopped mid-sentence to let it pass, which was about every fifteen minutes. It made the meeting rather disjointed, but they all just seemed to put up with it.

There were a few new faces mixed in with the familiar ones. All the children had grown since I was in the congregation in 1980, the babies to seven-year-olds, the toddlers to teens and the young teenagers to young adults; men and women, getting baptised, pioneering. Were they happy? Maybe some of them were living a blissful life in the Truth, absorbed in it from dawn to dusk. But I was certain there would be those that were leading a double life, doing the Witness thing for the right observers but at school or work they were different people. How long can a young mind live in such torment? Be two different people with two sets of guidelines to live by? What does that do to a child's development?

There were many nods of recognition from those that remembered me, some with added smiles, a few with hard stares as they recalled being told of my misdemeanour by some gossip or other. My returned greetings matched theirs. Whispers about Ray's death came to me occasionally from concerned ones. He'd certainly left his mark in this congregation – they couldn't speak highly enough of him and reassured me of the resurrection hope that was now possible because of Jesus's sacrifice. It was all very familiar.

It was nearly time for the meeting to start. I'd chucked out my songbook and I didn't have a Watchtower for today's study so I would have to borrow and share. But really, I was there for just the public talk. I was ready to soak up some spiritual food and let my heart absorb those comforting words. The opening song was one from the new song book and I didn't know it so mumbled my way through it. The talk was entitled, 'How to be Clean in an Unclean World." Once I'd heard the title announced I immediately thought it was written for me and felt my head lowering. I had to quickly tell myself that this was a *public* talk, a discourse for the public who have wandered in off the street or who are perhaps studying and don't know what Jehovah's Witnesses are all about. It wasn't aimed at me. *Lift your head up, girl, it's not all about you. You've paid for what you did so let that be an end to it.*

I sat through all those familiar words; immorality, filth, confession, worldly, guilty, repentance. I kept calm and constantly reminded myself to keep the past in the past and not allow these terms to get to me. To concentrate on the more positive aspects, that of forgiveness and moving forward. Nobody would care what I did three years ago. Surely they've forgotten all about it and anyway, although some gossip would have been spread around down here, the majority of people wouldn't have known about my misadventures. I hoped I wasn't lying to myself.

At the end of the meeting, I said the final 'Amen' and put my Bible back in my bag. Ginny, of course, rushed up to me, all excited.

"I said to Geoff after we'd seen you in the restaurant, I said, "Geoff, I just know Jess will turn up at a meeting soon," and here you are!" She made to give me a bug hug but I sat back down in my seat. I didn't want all this fuss. I searched around for Kathy and made my excuses to Ginny.

A firm hand squeeze from Kathy spoke a thousand words. She was proud of me for getting to a meeting and I knew she hoped I would continue attending. Some of their children were there, others were spending the weekend with friends in Brighton so would go to the meeting over there. I was excited to break the news about mum's love interest. Kathy would have planned a wedding reception for them before she'd reach her front door. "Yes, I heard. Your mum rang last week. She sounds very happy." I was gobsmacked that Kathy already knew.

Well, thanks, mum, I thought. Thank goodness Peter called me and I didn't have to find out from someone else. It made me angry to think that, although I wasn't disfellowshipped, mum was certainly treating me as if I was. I mean, was this not an important family development that she should be telling me herself? I wondered if I would be invited to the wedding, whenever that would be.

I attended the Sunday meeting for a few weeks – there was no point going to the Theocratic Ministry School on a Thursday as I had no intention of going back out on the ministry. That meeting was solely designed to teach Witnesses how to answer questions from the public, how to teach effectively and overcome any obstacles raised. It was basically a Sales meeting. A lot of the techniques taught were also used in the sales world – how to open a sale, how to engage your audience, find common ground, good listening techniques, how to wrap up and seal the deal.

I couldn't cope with all that. I needed to be replenished myself first before I could start encouraging others. Neither did I want to go to the Tuesday Book Study held at Kathy and Greg's; it was far too intimate. Ginny kept trying to get me to go the Thursday meeting using her sly tactics – she had a chocolate cake recipe she just knew I would love and would bring it along on Thursday. *Well, I won't be there, Ginny, so I'll get it on Sunday.*

Quite reluctantly, I rang mum. Congratulated her on getting together with Charlie and, not knowing how she would react, told her that I'd been attending the Sunday meetings for a while now. There was no change in her voice as she said, "well done," and I could hear the caution as she asked me if I was still seeing Will.

"Yes, mum, he's the love of my life. I wouldn't be without him. If Charlie treats you as well as Will treats me, I know you'll be very happy.

"Well, that's all well and good Jessica but you know it will cause you problems in the future."

Can't she just be happy for me, just once? It wasn't necessary to throw the issue of morality at me quite so soon. I knew that at some point it would be expected for Will and me to get married if I was to continue with the Truth. And everyone would hope for him to come along and eventually get baptised. I could picture it: invitations to tea, *Oh, yes, bring Will along, yes of course he's invited! Be lovely to get to know him.* Invitations to the congregation barbeque up on the Downs: *Hey, Will, give us a hand here would you, my barbeque skills are a little rough.* Get him involved, make him feel part of this big spiritual family. But the truth was, they wouldn't want his friendship. Not really. They'd only go so far with him. If he didn't react favourably towards their efforts to get him to baptism then it would be bye, bye Will.

Conditional love. A common JW trait.

I got off the phone with mum and felt the first pangs of a dilemma forming. Trust mum to throw reality in my face. Her words made me wonder why

I was even bothering with any of it. Did I feel better for going? Was I getting the spiritual nourishment I was searching for? I had to admit that yes, I was, somewhat. It felt right. It had a calming effect on me, knowing that I was pleasing God. That was the one thing I had to keep that in mind no matter what happened.

Ginny and her beige husband in his beige suit usually took seats in the row directly behind me - I guess they wanted to keep an eye on me, make sure I was looking up all the scriptures, following along in the Watchtower, paying attention. It was tempting to open a bag of sweets with noisy wrappers and turn round to offer them one. After almost every meeting either Ginny or Geoff enquired about Will. I thought at first that it was out of genuine concern but the more I thought about it I knew it was just them trying to get him to come along. Geoff gave me a car magazine to pass on to Will, a cut out from a newspaper about a photography competition, something they could hook him with. But I binned them. I wasn't going to stand for, or encourage, their false friendship.

Before I got the bus to each meeting I said a prayer. I tried to keep an open, positive mind about the things I was hearing through the sound system. My request that I could leave the past behind and listen from a new, more mature standpoint was working and I absorbed the spiritual food being served from a variety of public speakers. There was no doubt that some of the Brothers were natural orators who knew how to engage their audience.

During some of the talks I could have heard a pin drop, such was the concentration. Treasures from the Psalms, passages in the New Testament that referred directly to another passage in the Old Testament, some of these speakers were very skilled at drawing out nuggets of wisdom. Others were not so skilled, they spoke in a monotone, asked us to follow along in the book of Lamentations as they read chapter after chapter and I frequently found myself slipping off into another world during their talks - swimming or something equally pleasurable.

I soon started to actually enjoy the public talk regardless of the subject. I began to take notes. I filled a spiralbound notebook of particularly interesting bits that I could go back over later on. This was feeding my mind and my soul (whatever that thing was), and that old familiar feeling of something deeply spiritual and satisfying touched me in a way that nothing else ever did. I knew I was pleasing Jehovah by just being there, at His table, enjoying hearing His thoughts through the pages of the Bible.

My prayers were working. I was beginning to let go.

CHAPTER 11

"You're looking a bit better these days, Jess," remarked Sandy one day at work. How about drinks later on? Come back to ours straight from work, yeh?"

I didn't hesitate.

"Love to."

It was great to be in good company again. The last few weeks had been extremely difficult what with all the emotions and memories that had been dragged up. But now I was able to relax and be at peace with my thoughts a little more.

Fish and chips papers moved to one side on the table, we took our cokes and moved to the comfy seats and kicked off our shoes.

"You've been in a strange place recently, off on a different planet," remarked Ellie as she plonked her leg up on the footstool. "So, Jess, what's been going on? Come on, time to spill the beans."

I had no choice but to tell them about Ray, the whole story. Well, the story without all the religious stuff. There was no point trying to explain all that to them. They wouldn't understand. Ray's ending came as a shock to them. Their gentle words of sympathy were very comforting and reassuring, yet in a different way to those that came from the Witnesses. Sandy surprised me when she said she'd been raised by Mormon parents. She briefly spoke of life after death and our spirit and body being reunited at the resurrection. Quite different to the Witnesses' teaching but I listened to what she said. It was instinctual to switch off when someone started talking about their beliefs for fear of being mislead but I found what she was saying actually interesting, fascinating.

So, maybe Sandy would understand after all if I let her in on my upbringing. I'd like to hear how she manages her relationship with her parents and how they treat her and Ellie.

What was the Mormons' view of homosexuality? And sex before marriage? I knew that in most religions both are unacceptable, but my thoughts went to how those people are *treated*. Are they automatically ousted? Are they instructed to be ostracised by family and friends? Are they accepted as long as they don't try to influence others? I didn't know. That would be an interesting conversation at some point, but not tonight.

We watched Educating Rita on their new rented 36-inch Ferguson TV (with remote control). I was half-watching the film, but my mind kept wandering off to the situation I found myself in. I felt totally relaxed with these lesbian girls and I'd overcome my ingrained prejudice of them and their actions. What they did with their time and who they gave their love and affection to was none of my business. But now, as I sat here, certain scriptures popped up in my memory and I realised that I had a duty to inform them that God was not pleased with their behaviour. While they sat enjoying the film I was picturing Armageddon and those death-dealing fireballs raining down from heaven. And when the paradise comes, after Armageddon, they would be no part of it, Jesus was pretty clear about that. Murderers, thieves, adulterers, homosexuals, deceivers, drunkards – none of these would inherit God's Kingdom.

I couldn't bear the thought of my two friends perishing with the rest of the evil world. My eyes started to fill with tears. I yawned and rubbed my eyes hoping no one would notice the wetness I was wiping away.

And yes, Armageddon was coming very soon! That's a fact. We must be so close to the end of this wicked system now. I mean all the signs are there – wars, famine, earthquakes (not hurricanes), it's all happening on a large scale, just as Jesus said. If they don't stop what they're doing with each other in their bedroom they're going to be squished and I'll never see them again!

I could feel my heart racing in my chest. I coughed and patted my chest.

"Just going to get some water," I announced and took myself out to the kitchen. I leaned against the worktop and took some deep breaths. What's happening? I had to calm myself down and take my mind off such intense thoughts.

"You ok?" called Sandy.

"Yeh, just a tickle," I reassured her as I came back in the lounge. "Best be making a move really, it's getting late. I'll get a taxi, Sandy, if I can use the phone."

"Sure, go ahead. I can run you home if you like, it's no trouble."

"No, it's ok, you're all cosied up." I looked at the two of them curled around each other on the sofa. They loved each other dearly, that was clear to see. It was such a shame. "No need to go out in the cold."

It had been a good evening and I considered the girls my good friends now. We'd done quite a bit together and I felt bad that I hadn't confided in them sooner about Ray. I just didn't want to burden them with my worries. They'd told me off for not speaking up and, when we said our goodbyes, they chimed simultaneously: "that's what friends are for". Yes, they were my friends. And yet, somehow I have to show them that God doesn't approve of their behaviour. Do I truly have the same opinion about lesbianism as God does? Do I hate it? Or do I just want to ignore it in order to keep their friendship? Does that make me a hypocrite, then? This was so difficult!

I'd made some great friends since moving down here. Sandy, Ellie, Theresa, Neil, Dominic (I wasn't quite sure about him, though) and of course those two angels, Charlotte and Spencer who I adored. Many faces around the village were familiar to me, and we were on nodding, chatting terms. I felt part of a community. But deep inside I still felt so different to them. We had things in common at this point in time, because I had a life and hobbies, interests, a job, but there was still that element of the absence of childhood memories, no shared experiences. Christmas, Easter, birthdays, after-school clubs. None of that was automatic to me: hanging decorations, writing cards, buying an abundance of presents for one person, working as a team. It was all so alien. Nothing would ever change that.

That Friday Will picked me up from work on his way through. He did it occasionally and it was always a nice surprise. We picked up tea from the Chinese takeaway, enough for Esther too, and spent a cosy evening in front of the TV. The weather was horrible outside; assisted by a strong westerly wind the rain was battering the side door and fierce gusts blew plastic plant pots around the garden. Freezing temperatures and black ice had been forecast for the weekend ahead and that's what made Will decide to come over this evening instead of tomorrow morning.

"There's a few of us going out tomorrow night. Gulliver's this time. Thought it would be a change from Dixieland. Want to come?"

I didn't know many of Will's friends that well, but I knew they were a lively bunch. My immediate reaction was *yes, of course I want to come, why wouldn't I?* Then I remembered I had a meeting to go to the next morning. I couldn't get home too late as I'd be up and out to catch the bus at nine.

"Well, that's ok, we don't have to stay too long. Couple of hours at the most, yeh?"

Famous last words.

I was having a fabulous time with these clowns. Their antics made me cry with laughter right throughout the night. Even the doorman and bar staff were entertained with their dance moves. Needless to say I got absolutely wrecked and wasn't paying attention to the time. Will informed me in the morning that it was gone two when we left the club.

"Why didn't you take me home?!!" I blasted at him. "I've got to go to the meeting," I moaned as I tried to get up out of bed.

"Don't think you should go anywhere in the state you're in, my girl. Have a day off, for god's sake. Come back to bed."

"But they'll wonder where I am and they'll come knocking on the door and want to know exactly why I wasn't there. I'm trying to be good, Will." My head was pounding and I had one arm in my blouse when I flopped back on the bed and let sleep take me again.

"Are you decent?" Esther called at about one o'clock, "I've got tea."

"Come in," Will moaned.

Esther laughed as she looked at me. My hair was all over the place, I knew it, and there was mascara on the pillow.

"No meeting this morning, Jess?"

"No, and it's Will's fault. He kept me out too late."

"Well, it won't do you any harm to have a week off, I'm sure." She put the tray down on the dressing table and poured us each a mug of very welcome steaming hot tea. She was so thoughtful and considerate.

"Breakfast in twenty minutes," she called as she left, closing the door behind her.

My ears were ringing, mouth was dry and the tea was too hot to drink. I blew across the top of the mug.

I caught the first welcome whiffs of bacon and realised how hungry I was.

"How do you think you're doing with the meetings anyway, Jess? Is it turning out to be what you wanted? And how is everyone towards you?"

"Ugh, too many questions! Give me a minute. I need this tea."

Will hadn't questioned me about my new Sunday routine. He'd been very patient, just allowing me to do my thing in my own time. We still had plenty of time together at the weekends and some Sunday mornings he'd gone to the pool himself which he never did before.

I told him about how it all made me feel and different conversations I'd had with various ones. He thanked me that I hadn't passed on the motoring magazine and details of the photograph competition from Geoff. He would have known without me telling him that it was no more than a ploy to get him to "join the JW club" as he put it.

"He's a bit keen isn't he, that Geoff. Well, both he and Ginny are. They're so intense."

"Loads of people are like that in the Truth, Will. It's serious stuff, life and death. They talk about heavy subjects every day, answer people's questions. It's no wonder they don't know how to enjoy themselves. They aren't able to put all that aside for a moment, or long enough to let their hair down. Serious stuff indeed."

I decided to open up to Will about the return of a what appeared to be a mini panic attack the other night. I'd had several during the time I spent down here with Ray. It was just my guilty conscience, I think. A torrent of emotion my brain couldn't deal with and it manifested itself as hyperventilation and, at times, losing consciousness. I couldn't put up with all that again and really hoped this wasn't the start of not being in control of my emotions again.

"So, the girls didn't notice anything?"

"No, I managed to hide it from them, went out to the kitchen."

"Oh, Jess," Will sighed, taking another sip of his tea. I leaned my head against his shoulder and pulled the covers up around us.

"Jess, Jess, Jess. What am I gonna do with you?" He put his tea on the bedside cupboard and drew me closer.

We took a walk down to the Aqua Bar later on that day. There was a guitarist playing and a gentle, relaxed atmosphere down there. The coat stand was heavy with jackets and umbrellas and quite a number had braved the weather for a bit of entertainment on a Sunday evening. It was warm inside and we got a table by the bar away from the chill of the door.

"I don't believe it!" I looked to where Will was looking only to see you know who walking in.

"I told you, Will, I bet she asks why I wasn't at the meeting this morning."

They didn't see us at first and I thought we'd got away with it but no, as she turned round from the bar she looked me straight in the eye.

We were subjected to the usual over-enthusiastic greeting. I had to get ahead of her somehow. I was not prepared to answer her when she asked her question. My reason for missing a meeting was none of her or anyone else's business and I would not be accepting any display of 'concern'.

"Ginny, how come we always seem to bump into you two, then? Are you following us?!"

I made a joke of it but I wanted to know. It suddenly struck me that, yes, ok, Pevensey Bay was not a big place but for those two to keep popping up everywhere we went was a bit strange to say the least.

"Ah, it's a coincidence, isn't it? We just like the same places obviously. Mind if we…er…" and she pointed to the seats beside us. Thankfully someone from a neighbouring table came and swiped one of the chairs. I could have hugged him.

"Oh, well, we'll sit over there." She seemed to be distracted by another couple that had walked in and were heading for the same vacant table. "Missed you this morning, Jess. It was a lovely talk from Brother Logan. Geoff can you hang my coat up for me please." She put her bag down and shrugged off her bulky coat. As she did so, I saw something fall from one of the pockets. As Ginny darted across to another table before the other couple took it, I picked up the little book and was going to hand it back to her. That was, until I saw my name on the cover.

A quick flick through the pages of the A5 size notebook showed it was set out in a grid. Among the headings were: date, time, activity, place, my name, Will's name, a column for 'other'. What the hell was this? I couldn't work it out.

"What's this about? Will, look."

I saw his expression as he struggled to decipher the meaning and purpose of keeping such a record of our, mostly my, activities. As far back as April one entry read:

Walk or car? Car.
If car then alone or E there? Alone
Holding hands? Tick.
Arm around shoulder? Tick.
Time arrived at house: 7.05pm
Time left: prob stayed over. Checked following morning – car not moved.
Dress: very short skirt, high heels
Drunk? Yes probably as swaying and giggling

I held out my hand. "Here, give it to me. I'm going to find out what bloody game she's playing." I was so angry and bumped the table as I stood up sharply.

"No, wait, Jess. Wait." Will pulled me back by my sleeve. "This is spying, tracking, harassment. Why? What reason has she got for doing this? Any ideas?"

I sat back down and thought for a moment. Mum's words came back to mind, about my immoral lifestyle going to cause me trouble one day. And this was it. Ginny was gathering evidence.

"The bitch!"

"So, she's presumable going to hand this in to one of the Elders at some point. Drop you in it. And then what happens?"

"I've never tried to hide you, Will. Everyone knows you're part of my life. And they presume we're having sex. It's that simple. They don't ask, not that it's any of their business, they just presume. Oh, Will."

"I suggest we go home, get your diary out and check all the dates to see if they correspond. We'll read through the whole thing, be absolutely certain that it is what you think it is and take it from there."

In a daze I followed as Will got his coat on and headed out the door. I gave a final look back at the bitch by the bar. She waved goodbye in her usual cheery manner. I just stared at her and considered what I'd like to do to her and her weasel of a husband.

I ran upstairs and grabbed my diary from the bedside cabinet. It was only a small gold coloured Letts diary which I used for appointments, and upcoming events. We spent the next hour going through each entry in Ginny's book and checking it against mine for the same days. Boy! Those two had been busy! Was there nothing better they could have been doing with their time than following us? We discussed the times I'd seen them, going back months. That time they followed me back from the Aqua Bar along the beach. The Sunday afternoon on our walk back from the Castle Inn. The night Petra was barking on our night-time walk. That chat we had in the chemist's. When they bumped into us down at the harbour. Suddenly it all fell into place.

"I thought it was Dominic that was following me!"

"Dominic? Why?"

I told Will about the hand on the thigh and the hot spoon incident at the work's meal. And that ever since then he'd been strange with me. He knew where I lived because he was in the car when Sandy dropped me off. It just felt like he was trying to scare me or something. But it was Ginny all along. This so-called Christian woman, my spiritual Sister, my 'friend'. The woman who supposedly cared about my well-being and spirituality. Well, she cared so much it seemed she's going to report all my actions to those lovely, caring Elders. They'd be sure to set me straight, feed me the correct encouraging scriptures about not being immoral outside of marriage and that if I'm not completely on Jehovah's side then I'm on the side of the Devil. I knew that conversation was coming.

But part of me was enjoying the security that the meetings provided. It was something I'd been doing all my life and there were some aspects of it that I liked: the singing, praying together, hearing encouraging words, and uplifting personal experiences that people had. The chatter before and after the meetings, feeling that I belonged somewhere. The Elders would expect me to marry Will. If I didn't then that would show how shallow and weak my faith was, that I didn't want to worship God enough, that I didn't really want to be part of the only true Christian organisation. I knew they would put the choice before me, lay it on the table. The Truth or Will. And I would have to decide.

CHAPTER 12

Charlotte and Spencer were staying at Theresa's for the weekend. Their mum, Annabel, was attending a counselling session and needed some space and time on her own afterwards, so Theresa explained. She never minded having her niece and nephew over and said she viewed it as good practice for when she and Neil have their own kids. But this Saturday night they'd already booked tickets for the cinema and so asked me to babysit.

It was a bitterly cold day and, despite wearing two pairs of woolly gloves on my trip to the newsagent's to buy some treats for the kids, my hands were still frozen. Theresa picked me up at half six after I'd had tea. Will was out with his mates; they were going bowling then planned to have drinks at the Crown and Anchor. I felt privileged to be entrusted with the care of these children, to play with them, laugh with them, keep them safe. At bedtime, Spencer got comfortable under my arm and proudly talked me through his dinosaur book, taking his time over the long nose of the ichthyosaurus. Charlotte had dug out Mary Poppins from her overnight bag and showed me how well she could read. She was indeed, excellently expressive. I wondered if I'd ever get to cuddle up with my own niece and hear her reading skills.

I crept out of Charlotte's room and pulled the door to quietly, careful not to wake her. Once downstairs I took out the photo of Bethany I carried in my purse. She was such a cutie at six months old, but I had no idea what she would look like now. In that moment I made a decision: it was time to put pen to paper and write Peter a letter. I would have to be straight with him, ask him outright if I can arrange a time to see Bethany. I could do the journey in a day, that wouldn't be a problem. I would have to be a Saturday as, of course, as I wouldn't want to miss the meeting on a Sunday. Surely he would agree to a short visit?

Will turned up at Theresa's about eleven, just before they returned, and following a quick coffee and a chat we drove home.

I stayed up late writing, trying to find the right words, the correct tone - not too forceful, not too wimpish, and I wasn't going to beg. I let Peter know how I was enjoying going back to the meetings and that my faith was being renewed. The effects of the past were slipping away and being replaced with more positive thoughts and worthwhile activities. How could he refuse me contact with my niece? What more could I do than reassure him I was back on the right track? Perhaps I should start attending the Thursday night meeting. Get ready to go out on the Ministry again. Count my hours, place the Watchtower and Awake magazines, books and booklets and put in a monthly report. But saying that, it would encroach on the time Will and I have together as I'd have to go out on the ministry on a Saturday morning, so no more late Friday *or*

Saturday nights. But I'm sure Will would understand. And Peter would be pleased with my efforts.

The next day I posted the letter in the box at the end of the street. Now I knew who had been spying on me I wasn't so conscious when I went outside. By now Ginny must have noticed her book was gone. Well, let her panic, let her stew. She'll have nothing to pass to the Elders now, just the bits she can remember. As I dropped the letter into the box, I sent it with my hopes that Peter would be in a good mood when he read it and would call me or write back soon. I couldn't wait to see Bethany!

After the big storm my workload seemed to be settling down again, back to the usual level of post to open, paperwork to file and cover notes to write out and distribute. One Tuesday afternoon, just after lunch, Mr Roades called me into his office.

"It's been noticed, Jessica, just how well you coped with the extra work thrown up by the storm. We were all pretty snowed under, I can tell you, but for a Junior, you worked hard and appeared to deal with everything you were given to do. It may be time to think about some training in the business. Is that something you'd like?"

I didn't know what to say. Was this a... a... career coming my way?

"Well, Mr Roades, I'd really like that, thank you. I find the work interesting and varied. I never get bored here, and I'd like the opportunity to progress in the business, yes. What do you have in mind?"

"Eastbourne College are offering a two-day course in the Principles of Insurance, and on successful completion, can offer a one-year course in Insurance Foundation."

I smiled, feeling proud of myself. "That sounds very good, thank you."

"You'll do the two-day course during work time but the other one you'll do on Thursday evenings at the college. How does all that sound?"

Thursday evenings? Just my luck. Why couldn't they run it on a Tuesday? Or a Wednesday? Of course, I was presuming I'd get through the two-day course with no problems. Maybe I was jumping the gun.

"That sounds very good, Mr Roades. Thank you."

Will was very pleased for me, and Esther too.

"This is a great move, Jess. It could be the start of a very promising career for you. You're intelligent and these courses should be no problem for you. And most of it will be familiar. This is great news!"

I felt so excited and – another feeling that I couldn't remember having before – I felt worthy. Yes, Mr Roades was right, I had worked hard during that busy period and I'd coped with it all. Maybe I did deserve to go further. He was willing to invest his money in training me so he must think I'm capable. Here was someone putting their faith in me for a change and recognising my value. I was chuffed to bits!!

The next Sunday meeting I went to I sat near my usual place. Not exactly the same seat, but close enough. I didn't want to be one of those people who got shirty when someone else sat in *their* seat. A lot of the older ones seemed to do that – they just couldn't help themselves. Just like I couldn't help giving Ginny and Geoff the cold shoulder. There was actually, literally no way I could bring myself to speak to them. Each time Ginny began to head in my direction I turned and occupied myself with someone else, or rummaged in my bag, or put my coat on. I was so disgusted that they would do what they did. Were they expecting praise for their great detective skills? From the Elders? From God? Did they really believe they would be *saving* me by doing such a thing?

I spent the whole meeting quietly seething and couldn't concentrate on what was being said. I had to get my mind on the material and the best way to do that was to prepare an answer to one of the questions in the Watchtower. I hadn't answered up before and felt extremely nervous but I needed to think about spiritual things, not about Ginny and Geoff's antics.

The most nerve-wracking thing about the whole experience of answering up was using the microphone. Any young baptised Brother in good standing in the congregation could be given the privilege of handing out the mic to the raised hand selected by the speaker. I feared my mind would go blank in between the speaker saying, "yes, Sister Dalton," and me actually feeling the heavy cold metal in my hand. Thankfully I was sitting on the end of a row of seats so it shouldn't take that long. My heart was beating fast and my palm suddenly sweaty. I hoped I wouldn't drop the thing.

After the reading of paragraph eighteen, the study conductor asked the question: "According to the prophecies of Jesus and of Zechariah, what does a person have to do to be counted as one of Jehovah's "sheep"?

Anyone was capable of answering any question. All that was expected was a regurgitation of what was printed in the corresponding paragraph, you just needed to put it in your own words. There was no room, or encouragement, to add anything from your own thoughts, just the information printed in the magazine was sufficient. A child could do it, and they often did.

The mic was on its way. It was far heavier than I expected and it wobbled in my grip. "Zechariah chapter eight verse twenty-three says: "We will go with you people, for we have heard that God is with you people." So, we are not just friends with God's people, we, as the scripture says, "go with" them and become fully involved in Jehovah's organisation."

"Yes, thank you, Sister," and that was that. My racing heart settled down eventually, and my blushed cheeks regained their normal colour. But no sooner had I settled than my thoughts about Ginny returned.

I needed to walk. I needed to think.

Each meeting I attended, I expected to be called to one side by one of the Elders.

It was like waiting for a bomb to go off, a bullet to the chest, an arrow in the eye.

"Well, let's get married, then, Jess. If that's all that's standing in the way of you feeling completely at ease and escaping the wrath of those Elders, then let's do it."

He was just so sweet. This wonderful man whose eyes were the first I saw after regaining consciousness, lying on the grass outside the Beefeater Steak House three years ago. A rather severe panic attack had brought us together. I didn't deserve him. He was my treasure and my soul mate. But marriage….? No, it wasn't right. Being pushed into a corner was the wrong thing for both of us and I wasn't prepared to go down that road for anything other than the right reasons. I didn't want to run the risk of spoiling what we'd got. It was precious and I wanted to protect it. There were far too many couples I knew who'd jumped into marriage for the sake of having 'legitimate' sex – because, let's face it, that's all this boiled down to in the Witness world – and half of them didn't last beyond a couple of years. No. It's not happening with us.

I thanked Will profusely for his offer and explained my view of the whole thing. As usual, he understood and eventually agreed that it wouldn't be the best idea. He just wanted to make me happy, and I couldn't hold that against him.

My final Friday night out with Will and the girls was tinged with much sadness. Sandy and Ellie didn't know that I wouldn't be going out any longer, that I had God's work to do. Part of me felt embarrassed to tell them, another part of me wanted to explain the whole lot to them, warn them, invite them to a meeting, like I was supposed to do as a good Jehovah's Witness.

Dixieland was heaving. Bitterly cold outside, everyone was on the dancefloor trying to get warm. The wind howled through the gaps around the main door and late in the evening ice was forming on the outside of the windows. My throat was feeling a bit sore each time I swallowed, and no amount of lager was helping it. I changed to brandy – that's supposed to be medicinal, isn't it? By the end of the evening I couldn't tell whether I was drunk or feeling feverish and I just leaned on Will all the way back down to where he'd parked. We dropped the girls off, Theresa had come along too, and once I got into bed I was out like a light.

I woke at some point in the night with my throat on fire and my neck feeling like I'd swallowed a couple of tennis balls. I ached all over. Wrapping myself up I made my way down the stairs and got some Aspirin and took some careful, painful sips of water. Back in bed I snuggled down trying to get warm but the shivers wouldn't leave me.

Will took care of me the following day and I suggested he keep a distance between us in case he caught whatever this was. My appetite had disappeared and all I wanted to do was sleep. Fortunately, we had nothing too exciting planned for this weekend. Will wanted to go round to his mate's to watch the football but was worried about leaving me. I reassured him that I would be all right on my own as Esther was out at her sister's. Two more Aspirin took the edge off the chills, just enough for me to venture downstairs and warm up the thin soup

Esther had left for me. I tried to swallow some but my throat was too sore.

While sitting at the kitchen table I heard the phone ringing out in the hallway. It sounded louder than normal with my head already pounding. Covering my ears I wished it would stop. It probably wasn't for me anyway. Whoever was calling was very persistent as they tried again a couple of minutes later. I groaned and knew I'd have to answer it otherwise they'd just keep trying.

"Peter," I whispered.

"Jess, is that you? You sound different."

"I'm not well," I croaked down the line, hoping he would do all the talking.

"Ah, no, not got the dreaded lurgy, have you? Just wanted to say thanks for your letter. I read it through a few times and Janey read it too. We're both so pleased you've seen sense and are going back to the meetings. It's the only safe place to be, protected by Jehovah's loving organisation. You've done the right thing, Jess."

I wanted him to hurry up and tell me when I could see Bethany.

"How's Bethany?" I prompted, trying to get him closer to the point of this conversation. I felt a wave of weakness wash over me and set myself down on the bottom stair. A cold sweat broke out on my forehead.

"She's very well, growing so fast. Let's make a date and get together, shall we?"

Yes!

He had lots to do the following two weeks but the weekend after that they were coming down to see

Kathy and Greg for the day. It couldn't be better. I'd get to spend the day with my family and play with my beautiful niece. So there it was. A firm plan. I couldn't wait to see her cute face and feel her little arms around my neck.

I took myself back up to bed and although I felt like death at least now I had something exciting to fix my thoughts on. I would go into town next Saturday and buy her some presents, maybe a new dress, a toy. I'd have to ask Kathy what three-year-old girls like to wear and play with as I had no idea.

Maybe this was the start of getting things back into my life. Valuable things, like family, that I should never have been separated from in the first place. As for dad and my sisters, well, I didn't see any kind of relationship with them now. They lived so far away and too much time had passed by to catch up on all that we'd done in our lives. It was too late.

I got through my cold despite it taking over a week to feel back to normal. It wasn't flu, just a cold, and I had to keep correcting those at work who gave me extra sympathy and told me how bad they'd felt when they'd had it. I'd managed not to take any sick days and part of me was pleased, but when Dominic went down with the same thing at the end of the week I felt I was to blame.

Getting ready to go out on the ministry was something I hadn't done for over three years and it felt strange. It was freezing right now and so I wore several layers under my coat. The meeting place was at the house of John and Sylvia, a elderly couple, in

Langney at 9.30am. I hadn't prepared anything to say and I planned to ask if I can be paired up with Sylvia as I knew she liked to do all the doors herself. It was cheating a bit, I suppose, but this was my first time and I felt quite out of my depth. In my bag I had my Bible and two sets of the latest magazines just in case I got brave and wanted to do a door or two.

All at the group were pleased to see me out and as we walked through the pathways to the designated Closes to work, we chatted and laughed at John's big Russian fur hat. He didn't care, he was warm. This was familiar territory. I remember working these streets years ago, hoping that none of my school mates were at home behind these doors. I had the same worry now but considered that, like me, they might have moved away.

I got through the hour in the freezing temperatures and by the end, couldn't feel my feet. My long boots were warm around the legs but my toes were like ice. I needed to buy some furry insoles. The gap between the top of my boots and the hem of my skirt allowed the bitter wind to run up my thighs. A slip, tights, two pairs of knickers and I was still frozen. Only trousers were the most practical things to wear in this weather but, no, Sisters were not allowed to wear trousers. Men were to look like men, and women like women. That's what the Bible said, and the Governing Body was sticking to that rule. Funnily enough, it was deemed acceptable for trousers to make an appearance whilst working on a Quick Build site. All those Kingdom Halls that had been hurriedly built because the Organisation was expanding at such an alarming rate. Yes, all the

Sisters in the brick chains were wearing trousers! I guess it was all right for them to look like men on those days.

To thaw out we all piled back to Kathy's for a hot drink and crumpets. She put the fire on and we huddled round it until our red noses disappeared. I took the opportunity to talk to Kathy about Peter and Janey's visit.

"It'll be a lovely day, Jess. Be nice to see you and Peter here together after so long. He's missed you, you know. It's been hard for him not to get in touch with you all this time. You see, he wanted you to come to your senses and was convinced you would do it, in your own time. He wanted to be part of the reason you came back and if he'd always associated with you well, then you might never have made the move."

I snorted in disbelief.

"I can sort of understand that Kathy, but the reason I came back was because I needed some spiritual food and to be comforted after hearing about Ray's death. Peter had nothing to do with it and really, to come back just because someone wants you to, is not the right reason. Well, I'll let Peter believe what he likes, that his ostracism has worked. Perhaps he needs to believe that he's done the right thing."

We continued discussing the plans for Peter's visit. I would get there at about mid-morning to help with the food and they were due to arrive about one. Kathy said she could give me some of the kids' old toys to pass on to Bethany but I insisted that I would buy her a new outfit. Something green I think, to go with her gorgeous ginger hair. I wondered what length it would be. Curly or straight? In a ponytail or loose? Maybe I should get Will round to take some good quality photos of her.

Wait! What am I thinking? Of course I can't invite Will! My fornication partner, my worldly boyfriend. Peter would press us to talk about a wedding, he'd bring the conversation round to the Truth and would try to set up a weekly study with Will and Greg. That could really spoil the day. No! I'm not having that. Will just won't be able to come. I'll bring my own camera and take some snaps throughout the day.

"You know it's not only Jehovah's Witnesses that don't agree with sex before marriage," said Esther out of the blue that evening. She must have been thinking about the situation I found myself in and Will would have told her of his proposal.

"Take a look at Christianity in general. Most religions don't approve of it, it goes back centuries. The Romans had a marriage ceremony to legalise property, wealth and to secure a future for any children that came along. The same in Tudor times, Victorian times. And it was accepted. If a couple didn't formalise their union, well, the woman, and it was always the woman, would lose out on any practical benefits."

"Interesting. But today we don't have to be married to live together. It's not a legal requirement and, as for the stigma of having a child out of wedlock, like in the sixties, it's just not like that these days. Personally, I think it was more to do with the fella making sure everyone in the town knew who his property was. The woman had no rights and everything that would have been hers went to the husband. It's a man thing. Will? Any thoughts?"

"This is not quite the angle you're coming from though, Jess, is it?"

"What do you mean?"

"Well, your lot say that it's *God* who says you must be married before indulging in….in.. you know… and yet, as you've pointed out before, Adam and Eve didn't have a wedding ceremony. They were simply bound together before God and told to stay together. It's politics that's brought about all the rules and regulations and traditions. That's what I think anyway."

"Mmm. I don't know. I don't even want to think about it. It's all too intense. All I know is my conscience is not bothered one iota about our marital status. So what does that say? I can't make myself feel guilty, guilty enough to rush down the registry office with you, Will. Anyway, what's for tea, Esther? Shall I cook tonight?"

CHAPTER 13

Christmas was coming and we could get lots of good deals if we hurried - so the store announcer in Tesco's said.

Last Christmas I spent with mum as I didn't want her to be on her own. It was the one time of year that she actually, literally hated. The whole thing from mid-December to the beginning of January seemed just so long to her and there was really nothing to do. I despised it too. No parties, of course, no Christmas shopping to do, no friends coming round for drinks. It was a period of intense nothingness and the only activity that any of us could be involved in was going from door to door, and that included on Christmas day itself. Well, that was the best time to catch people in, obviously. Many householders were more than happy to stand at the door and chat about spiritual things and were generally more friendly, being full of the Christmas spirit. Others would invite us in for a mince pie and a glass of mulled wine which was quickly declined of course. To accept would have been to condone what they were doing, and we couldn't be seen to be doing that. There were others still who took great pleasure in telling us to "piss off". The instruction seemed to be extra loud. I don't blame them, really.

Who wants to be interrupted when they've just sat down to a big family meal?

So, this Christmas I was going to get a better idea of what this worldly celebration was all about. Not that I would be taking part, no, I was doing well back in the fold and wouldn't want to be caught by the likes of Ginny Peacock out partying with worldly people and involving myself in pagan activities. I couldn't risk it. Not now I was getting my family back.

At work there was a different atmosphere the closer this big day came. It felt like there was a huge expectation of something wonderful floating about the office. The ones who didn't normally smile were giving cheesy grins and offering to make tea. A green plastic bag sat on a chair in the corner and every morning staff put cards and wrapped presents in there to be handed out on the last working day. A memorandum came round to everyone stating that on Thursday 24th Dec we would finish at 3.30pm to have drinks and nibbles in the kitchen.

What did I need to do? Buy cards and presents for everyone? That would cost a fortune! I could guarantee that Esther and Will would buy me Christmas presents, too. Yet another decision to make. Do I return the gesture? What about Sandy and Ellie, too? I really didn't want these special people in my life to think bad of me.

What *should* I do, being a member of a religion that disapproves of Christmas? If I gave no one a card or present they would all think I was a tight-fisted misery guts that didn't want to have any fun. I pictured myself at the counter in WH Smith's with a packet of cards smothered with the face of Santa Claus and reindeer and elves, baubles, tinsel and Christmas pudding. What if I got spotted by another Witness? I really don't want to upset anyone in the office, they're a good bunch and they've been very supportive of me since I started here. I really didn't know what to do.

Lots of plans were being made: Will had about three parties to go to over in Brighton, Esther was going to have all the family round on Christmas day for dinner. Sandy and Ellie had invited Will and I to two parties on 11th and 18th, both would be late finishers, I just knew it. Theresa and Neil had been asked out to dinner by some friends and wondered if I wouldn't mind babysitting on Sunday 20th as they were sure the children would be staying with them that night. I was more than happy to. An invitation even came from Dominic, of all people, to drinks and snacks at his friend's house in Willingdon. He'd been a bit more open and friendly lately. More like how he used to be before the hand on the knee misunderstanding. That might be a nice event to go to, if only to see what his friends were like. I imagined them as kind but a bit geeky.

Esther and I held the ladder while Will climbed into the attic and retrieved the box of decorations. They looked like they'd been thrown in with no folding or rolling up, bits of Sellotape still stuck to the ends and the batteries in the dancing Santa had run out. It all needed checking and hanging. And then there was the tree. It was six feet tall, plastic-wrapped branches folded upwards, four slide-on legs in a separate bag. Will slid it through the hatch to Esther's outstretched arms.

"I don't care if it's too early, this lot is going up tomorrow. The wreath, Will, where's the wreath for the front door?"

"How would I know? You dismantled everything last year. Probably in the bag with all the baubles."

The turkey had to be ordered at the butcher's no later than 7th December, which was this Monday. The final shop before all the shops closed would need to be done on 23rd because Duncan was arriving on 24th and he wanted to do some last minute present shopping so there wouldn't be time. Esther's sister Gail was bringing around her sack of gifts at 5 o'clock on 22nd and to help with a final clean of the downstairs and to check there was enough serving dishes.

So much to do!

But it was all to do with Christmas. And if I wanted to be a true Christian, I really shouldn't get involved in any of it.

Boxing day. What was that one all about? I had no idea why it was called that and didn't yearn for any kind of explanation. But this one was special – that was the day Peter, Janey and Bethany were coming to visit. That was the day I was looking forward to, more than any other. I couldn't wait to see my family again after so long.

I had to forego Top of the Pops from now on. Back to a two-hour meeting every Thursday night.

That was a sacrifice that really hurt. The first Thursday meeting I attended there was a talk entitled: "Witnessing as a Family During December." As soon as I heard the word "family" my attention reduced by half. But the matter of going out on the ministry across the three Christmas days was discussed, and the ministry groups would be meeting at 10.30am instead of the usual 9.30am. "Consideration should be given to householders who are sleeping late on any of the holiday mornings," the Brother told us. Mmm, that was something, I suppose. Still, I didn't see myself going out on those days.

I sat watching the two Sisters on the platform giving a five-minute role-play demonstration on how to answer difficult questions. I'd done that myself many times as a youngster. Sample questions were taken from the *Reasoning* book* or the *Live Forever** book and some Sisters made it sound so easy. Do your introduction, listen to the householder's response or objection. Remember to read the appropriate scripture out loud and hey, Bob's your uncle, let's start a Bible study! It was never that simple. I wasn't really looking forward to preaching again – it was a most unnatural thing to do – but it was part of a Christian life. How could I hope to be spared at Armageddon if I kept the Kingdom message all to myself and didn't warn people? Jesus told his followers to go out and make disciples of people all over the world. It had to be done and I knew that with sincere, heartfelt prayers and help from others on the day I would get through it.

The closer Christmas came the more confused I felt. There was so much that I wanted to be part of – all the parties and gatherings, present-giving and meals out – but I knew I had to make a decision. To have a clear conscience I had to make my mind up whether I was going to go to some, go to all or go to none.

I knew I would feel so guilty by attending any one of these plans. It was easy to tell myself that, "it's only a meal, it's only a party, you've been to parties before. Where's the harm in giving your friends a couple of presents?" But the fact remained that none of these events would be taking place if it wasn't for Christmas.

By way of a refresher, I ran through the reasons that Jehovah's Witnesses don't celebrate Christmas. Amongst others there was the fact that Jesus didn't instruct his disciples to do such a thing but rather put emphasis on observing his death and sacrifice. A pagan Roman festival took place on the same date way before Jesus was even born and when he came along, instead of worshipping the *sun*, they worshipped the *son*. But for all these legitimate reasons there was so much fun to be had and I didn't want to miss any of it! I bet half the people out there don't even believe in Jesus and yet they're having a fabulous time. That just wasn't fair!

And yet how could I party till four in the morning, get drunk, sing all the Christmas songs in the charts, and then go out on the ministry and explain to someone why we don't get involved in Christmas celebrations? That would make me a complete hypocrite. As the days passed and I pondered over all these thoughts I was leaning more to one side than the other. It was either all or nothing. I had to talk to Will.

As we sat in the lounge after lunch, he let me know what he thought of my decision.

"None?! You mean not even one party?"

"I can't, Will, I'm sorry. I'll eat by myself on Christmas day, I don't mind. Just tell your family I'm out somewhere – at Theresa's or something."

"Don't be ridiculous, Jess. There's nothing wrong with you eating a meal with us. We're not going to be slaughtering animals or sacrificing children. It's just a meal."

Even to my own ears, my plan to keep away from all of it sounded unbalanced and quite selfish.

"So, what am I going to tell Sandy and the others as to why you're not going to their parties? As a matter of fact, I think it should be *you* that tells them. You do realise how hurt they'll all be, don't you?"

"I'll explain. I'll make them understand that it's not personal. That I'm trying to do the right thing. They all know how commercialised Christmas has become anyway. I'm surprised how people allow themselves to get so sucked in."

"Be careful how you word things, Jess. Remember, these are your friends. New friends. You don't want to alienate them. You haven't got many."

That stung.

I turned away and busied myself with the Radio Times. There might be some good films on over the holiday.

"I'm sorry. That came out all wrong. Promise me you'll just give it some more thought, Jess, before you decide for sure."

"I've made my mind up, Will."

Esther was a little more understanding but she seemed a bit sad too.

"But you'll be on your own when all your friends are out enjoying themselves. You love a party."

"Don't worry about me, Esther. Hey, I'm used to being on my own at this time of year, aren't I?" It was true. Quiet, empty Christmases were all I'd ever known.

Boxing day was fast approaching. I'd stopped off in town on the way home from work on Friday as the shops were open till eight and I bought Bethany a gorgeous new outfit. A green velvet dress with a matching little bolero. I spotted a pair of long socks too that would go perfectly. They had a green bow at the top. It was just what I'd pictured, and I couldn't wait to see her in it. Only one more week at work and I'd been seeing her.

There was an atmosphere of winding down in the office during that final week. During the week between Christmas and new year only the boss needed to go in to check on things - everyone else had the whole week off. I was ready for a break. I loved my job but sometimes I could do with switching off and doing something different. I had three weeks' paid holiday to take so in the new year I would take some days off and do some day trips to

London or go and see mum. Maybe I could stay at Peter's and spend some proper time with Bethany.

At work I grabbed Sandy and asked if I could go round straight from work, there was something I needed to tell her. She looked a bit confused and curious but said yes that's fine. During the afternoon, in between phone calls and filing schedules I had to figure out the best way to explain why I wouldn't be going to their party.

Ellie was already home when we walked through the door and the kettle was on.

"Better sit ourselves down, Ellie, Jessica here has something important to tell us." Sandy whispered conspiratorially. Ellie played along and they both sat on the edge of the sofa like two little children, knees together, arms folded, waiting for me to start.

I was nervous. This wasn't easy at all and I sighed as I finished my speech. Sandy took the sting out of it as much for those two as for myself.

"You'll be back."

"What? No, no I won't Sandy. I'm afraid this is what I want long term and I can't be leading a double life. I'm so sorry, and you know it's not personal. You and Ellie have been such good friends to me."

I also took the opportunity to explain that I wouldn't be able to go out for late nights at Dixieland or any other clubs on a Friday as I needed to have had and enough sleep and a clear head to go out preaching the following Saturday mornings. Also the meetings on Sunday meant the same, no late nights out.

No, they didn't really understand. How could they? There were a few awkward silences and then Sandy piped up again:

"As I said, you'll be back."

And there the conversation ended. We drank tea and chatted like normal after that and I ended up staying for dinner. Ellies' spag bol was getting more and more tasty each time she made it. I was really going to miss these girls – their funny ways, their kindness and understanding, their support, and especially would I miss Sandy's straight way of dealing with things. But I told myself, I'd still see them from time to time but the nights out would have to stop for me.

Explaining to the girls was one thing but I didn't know how to get round the problem that would arise at work. What would happen when, on the last Friday, the green bag was emptied and I'm handed cards and presents? There would be none from me in return. People would notice pretty quickly, I would imagine. Perhaps I should make my excuses and leave early. Avoid it altogether.

That's what I did in the end. I couldn't face the embarrassment and told a pack of lies about having to leave as Will and I have somewhere to be. Really sorry, have a great week off! Bye, everyone! I couldn't bring myself to say: "Merry Christmas". That was definitely off the menu.

No, I shouldn't have done it. Telling lies, for one thing and then sneaking off. I should have been bold enough to explain. But I wasn't. It was easier just to disappear.

Esther kindly plated up a lovely roast dinner for me and I warmed it up when I got back from my beach walk. I thought I'd give the family time and space to do their Christmas thing without me being around. As I sat eating at the kitchen table nobody asked me any questions so I guessed Esther must have said something. I bet they all thought I was weird and stuck up. If I'd been an onlooker I might have thought the same. I was quite glad they didn't question me though. I'd done enough explaining.

Laid out on my bed was a scattering of cards and presents. I recognised Will's handwriting and Esther's but there were others there too. I read through the sweetly worded cards and appreciated the sentiments inside. But looking at the presents I felt an immediate bolt of guilt and couldn't bring myself to open them. They were beautifully wrapped in shiny foil paper and each one had a satiny bow on top. So much care had gone into choosing and presenting these gifts. And I had nothing for Will's family in return. Nothing. I made my mind up to buy presents in the January sales for each person who'd thought of me, but still, I couldn't open these ones right now. I put them in a bag and placed them out of sight in the wardrobe.

I had to think about tomorrow – boxing day – and what I was going to wear and take with me to Kathy's. I'd got Bethany's outfit in my bag, the chocolate cake I'd made was downstairs in the pantry. I stuck to jeans and trainers, thinking that would be best for taking her out to the play park opposite the house. The heavy rain recently had made a mud pie of anywhere not paved and I hoped Janey had dressed Bethany appropriately. She couldn't expect her to be cooped up all day.

My beautiful niece! My flesh and blood. At last. The following day couldn't come soon enough.

CHAPTER 14

I stood by the window in Kathy's front room stretching my neck to spot their arrival. The trees had been stripped of their last few leaves as the wind had picked up last night and the ground had a shimmering white glow as the frost didn't want to leave. It was quarter to one and still freezing with no sun around to take the edge off the bitterness of the day.

A few of Kathy's kids were here, the ones that were still living at home and, surprisingly, my old friend Nerys had turned up. She'd driven down from London yesterday as the roads were quiet and had planned to stay till Tuesday. Her rather quick marriage was still intact – well, she was still wearing her wedding ring, at least. I must find a quiet space and have a proper chat with her, see how she's really doing.

One o'clock came and went, half past, quart to two. Finally at half two I saw their car pull up outside behind Greg's Rover. I squealed and ran to the door. Peter had sent Bethany on ahead through the gate and as she ran towards me I held out my arms ready to swoop her up. But she just stood there in front of me. I realised she didn't actually know me. Nevertheless, I gave her a little kiss and introduced myself. Hearing her attempts at saying my name melted my heart and realising "Jessica" was a bit of a mouthful for her I just asked her to call me "Jess". Her voice was light and flowery, sweet and….ooh just divine. I could have eaten her all up.

Peter looked well, so did Janey and following kisses and hugs we settled in the lounge where the chatter started. The loud buzz of the initial "how are you"s melted into more detailed talk of the welfare of common friends, mum's engagement, Janey's new part-time job. I wondered who would be looking after Bethany while she was at work. Maybe her sister who lived nearby. As they continued, with Joan sitting in her usual chair, quite oblivious to her surroundings, I found I was only half listening. Kathy had given me a bag of toys for Bethany and I was content to play with her on the mat in front of the guarded fire.

Her hand/eye coordination was good and she knew her shapes – placing the correct brick in the right slot was no problem for her. Perhaps she had the same toy at home. She took to the brightly dressed dolly and kept her by her side regardless of what she was playing with. She stroked her long blonde hair and kept taking off and replacing her shoes. She asked me if the doll had a bag but I couldn't find one. She seemed happy to stick with one toy for quite a long time and then move on to another. As I danced the dolly around her she followed with her eyes but no amount of silly posing or gymnastic movements made her laugh. She was very quiet.

Occasionally she looked up at the adults and seemed to be listening to what was being said, taking it all in. Then she went back to her toys. A solemn girl, a thinker.

We had the buffet lunch out in the dining room and Bethany sat so nicely at the table. The rest of us milled around the room, there not being enough chairs. Greg asked Peter to say the prayer and during the sombre stillness I opened my eyes to see what Bethany was doing. Her little hands were clasped, fingers laced together under her chin and eyes tight shut. They'd trained her well. The younger kids sat near her and helped her with her food.

Following lunch, I asked her if she'd like to go for a walk. I was pleased to see her placed in a pair of Wellies, hat and gloves. A little playtime over at the park would do her good. She can let off some steam over there. The other kids came along too and as we carefully crossed the slippery road, Bethany holding my hand tight.

Swings and a slide, a roundabout and a rocking horse. I expected her to run around in a hurry to try them all but she stood and waited, as if expecting to be told where to go first. The others were off in a flash, laughing and shouting to each other.

"Come on Bethany, want to go on the rocking horse with me?" I encouraged her.

"Dess, hold my hand," she instructed me as we approached the long metal creature, its red plastic seats all lined up. I placed her in the one in front of me and wriggled to get the thing going. It was impossible, it was so heavy. Toby was the strongest out of the boys so I called to him: "Toby, can you push us!" and he got us bumping and thumping and nearly falling off. I had to hold on to Bethany somehow as well as try not to slide off myself. After only a short while she started to twist round and I shouted to Toby to stop. Throughout the whole ride Bethany didn't really look as if she was enjoying it. She didn't giggle, laugh or say anything. I thought it a bit strange. I'd brought my camera and took a few snaps of her. When I asked her to smile, she did, which was something, I suppose.

The same reaction came with all of the rides – the swings, even when we went really high; the roundabout didn't thrill her at all; the slide, as high as it was, didn't excite her enough for her to want a second go.

I wondered if it was because she didn't really know any of us, maybe a bit of shyness was the reason for her odd behaviour. But deep down, and I didn't like to form such a thought, I wondered if Peter and Janey were already being too strict with her. Yes, being taught from birth how to sit still for hours on end at meetings and assemblies produced great school pupils; the ability to take in large amounts of information will help her no end throughout her life. She didn't speak unless she was invited to speak, just as it is at the meetings. But at such a young age I could see she was not just obedient but inhibited.

It wasn't normal for a three-year-old not to giggle, squeal with delight at something funny, do role play with toys, play openly with other children and run around in total freedom at the park. Not normal at all. What could I do about it? How could I save my niece from being indoctrinated in the same way I was? The truth was, absolutely nothing. A conversation with Peter would be taken as interfering in their parenting methods. He would say, this is exactly how children should be raised in the Truth – to be obedient and to put the Truth first in their lives. But it was unbalanced, and it was only now that I could see it, looking in from practically the outside and with older eyes.

I made my mind up that I would do my best to always be there for her and to offer a listening ear when she gets older. Maybe she will take to the Truth, get baptised and really live the life her parents want for her. But maybe she will want something different and turn her back on it all and exercise her freedom to choose. But something worse than either of those alternatives would be if she lived a double life, torn right down the middle. Wanting to please her parents and everybody else but inwardly screaming to be allowed to think for herself and be her own person. A terrible dilemma which many Witnesses lived with, I'm sure.

When we got back from the park it was time to have something to warm us up. Kathy's solution was warm orange squash. I took a sip from one of the kids' glasses and found it to be disgusting. I opted for a steaming cup of tea instead.

Peter beckoned to me as the kids and Bethany got on with their own things. We sat in a quiet corner of the dining room and a sudden air of investigation fell heavily around me. He was going to ask about Will, I just knew it.

"So, Jess, how's things? I hear you've been offered some training at work."

"Yes, everything's good at the moment, Peter. My training starts in the new year and from what people have said it's based on what I've already been doing so shouldn't be too difficult."

"That sounds great. You could make a career out of it. Is that what you want?"

"Well, I have to support myself. I can't live with Esther forever. I'll need to earn enough to rent somewhere of my own at some point, won't I?"

"There are options, though Jess. Perhaps you *could* stay at Esther's long term. You could reduce your hours and go part-time. Pioneer. Don't forget that's your ultimate goal, putting the Kingdom first."

Oh, give it a rest, Peter. I've not long started going back to the meetings. Stop putting pressure on me.

"Wouldn't you like to pioneer, Peter? You know when money's short Jehovah would provide everything you need. Why don't you give it a go? *Goose, gander.* Is Janey pioneering at the moment? I heard she's got a new job. What's she doing?"

"Yeh, she's in Marks and Spencer's for three mornings a week. She loves it. Gets twenty per cent discount on everything, too. Thing is, she was asked to work till eight on the three late shopping nights leading up to Christmas but she turned it down because it was on Thursday nights. I was really proud of her. They really put pressure on her but she stuck to her guns." His face had a look of wistful pride as he considered how dedicated Janey was.

"And what do you think of mum's news? Bit of a surprise, I must say." Peter was very protective of mum and understood her mental problems well. Now that he would be handing over her care to someone else must be a bit concerning for him.

"As long as Charlie can stand her mood swings they'll be just fine, I think. I need to go up and have a chat with him. I mean, I remember Charlie as being a very gentle bloke and he'll be good for mum, but I just want to make sure he knows what he's taking on. She can be a handful at times as we know."

A moody bitch, that's more the phrase I had in mind.

"Perhaps we should go up together. Make it clear that he needs to look after our mum properly, or else!"

"Yeh, I'll wear a mac and keep my hand in the inside pocket. Give him something to think about!"

We had a laugh about it and shared some memories about Larry, Greg's younger brother and how life might be now if he and mum had got together.

"Nah, it wouldn't have worked. I mean, look at Larry now, he's huge. His health and mobility are in a serious state. There's no way mum could have coped with that."

I'm still waiting, Peter. Just get to what you really want to talk about.

He shuffled in his chair and wrung his hands.

"Sooo, Will. How's Will doing?"

"He's very well, thanks. You must meet him some day. You'd get on like a house on fire."

"What does he do for a living?"

"Freelance photographer. He gets commissions all over the south-east and in London. He's very good at what he does and has had some of his work in glossy magazines and exhibitions. And the best thing is – he loves his work. I could see him doing that for the rest of his life."

I wanted Peter to know how stable Will was, how content. When the appropriate moment came I would also be showing him how much he loves me and how protective of me he is. How much fun we have together. How good he is to his mum and his family. How much he likes to have a laugh but knows when to be serious. Also - and this would mean a lot to Peter – how well he understands and accepts my desire to be back in the Truth.

"Well, that's all well and good, Jess. He sounds perfect. But you know what I'm going to say don't you?"

"Yes, I do, but don't, please." I stood up and moved over to the window. The light was beginning to fade as the grandfather clock chimed four. "There's no point, Peter, I don't need to hear it." But he carried on.

"You have a simple choice to make. Marry him or give him up. You can't serve two masters, as the scripture says. You can't continue to lead an immoral life and profess to be a Christian."

"Stop it!" I almost yelled at him.

But I knew he was right.

I looked around for Nerys. It was time to have that chat with my old friend. She was leaning against the wall as all the seats were taken, and seemed to be miles away, lost in her own thoughts. She looked a bit pale, I thought. Sliding my arm through hers I lead her out to the kitchen. She'd changed her hairstyle from blonde with auburn streaks to dark brown, dead straight and all the same length. And she'd started wearing glasses.

"All right, Specky? What's with the glasses? Didn't know you needed help with your eyesight."

She took off her slightly tinted frameless glasses and looked me directly in the face, unsmiling. My mouth fell open as I saw what she didn't want to be seen. The white around her left iris was completely red, and the same but a little less vivid in the right. The skin above her left eye was puffy and bruised. She looked like she'd stepped out of a horror movie.

"What the hell?" It was her husband Ritchie, I knew it. Never having met the man I had no solid reason to presume he was responsible for the state of Nerys's face but who else could it have been? They'd been pushed into getting married young, both were baptised Witnesses and under pressure to marry or risk being disfellowshipped if they'd jumped into bed. Perhaps he was now regretting it.

She replaced her glasses and explained that he'd developed a drinking problem and didn't try to hide it. He didn't show much remorse it seemed and had been disfellowshipped once the Elders found out what he'd done to her.

"What do his parents say? They must know why he's behaving like this. And how long has it been going on, Nerys?"

"Since not long after we got married. They can't control him. They've tried. No one can. I've made him appointments to see someone from Alcoholics Anonymous but he won't go. I don't know what else I can do."

"You can pack your bags and come back down here to your parents' that's what you can do." Why was she still with him after three years of abuse?

"But I can't leave him, can I? We're married and I made vows to him. He's my husband. I've talked to mum about the situation and I have to stick it out, try not to upset him and hope he settles down. I'm sure it's just a phase."

"You're bloody nuts, Nerys! Wake up! He's not going to stop. Or he may well stop for a while, but he'll turn on you again and it will just go on and on. You're in danger, can't you see that?"

"I know. It's not been just mum and Greg, the Elders have shown me that it's my duty to stay with my husband and be loyal to him. If I stay loyal to him then that means I'm being loyal to Jehovah too."

"I think I know the answer, but is he going to any meetings now?"

"No, I go on my own. He stays at home."

"And how is he with that? He's not trying to stop you going, is he? Because if he is endangering your spirituality then you have every right to leave him. I heard that once at an assembly. They said that the only way a wife could leave a violent husband is if he stops her going to meetings."

"Well, no he doesn't stop me going. Actually, he's pleased to get rid of me for a couple of hours. He can drink in peace without me having a go at him."

I could see a darkness come over her face as she looked down into her lap.

I reached over to cover her hand with mine.

"And what's he like when you get back?"

Nerys suddenly burst into tears.

"That's when he gets nasty. He asks me loads of questions about all the people there, what happened, what they said. Did anyone ask why he wasn't there? Did I tell his friend Dave what he thought of him for ignoring him the other day at the garage? Then he just works himself up into a rage and blames me for all that's wrong in his life."

She sobbed as I took her in my arms.

"No one has told me to leave him, except people at work," she snuffled. "I don't talk to them about it. I don't want their advice. All my friends, mum, Greg, Ritchie's parents, the Elders, everyone tells me I have to stay with him. Except you."

"Do you *want* to leave? Forget about what you think you should do as a good little Witness wifey. Do you want to stay in that situation forever?"

I thought her wailing reply of "Noooo!" was loud enough to get someone running to see what had happened. She sobbed and sobbed with her face in her hands and I didn't try to stop her.

"My eye is killing me, Jess. The socket is fractured and there's nothing the doctor can do about it. I keep taking painkillers, that's all." It looked so swollen and sore.

"Oh, for goodness sake, Nerys."

She talked and rambled and the words just tumbled out as if she'd been keeping them locked up for a long time. She thought Ritchie had an affair but had no real solid evidence and, of course, when she told the Elders about her suspicions was reprimanded for repeating what only amounted to a rumour.

She stayed close to me for the rest of the day and seemed subdued understandably. I was cross with Kathy and Greg for giving her such poor advice and wondered if they would actually allow her to come back and live here. But that was for them to discuss and decide. I assured Nerys I would always be there for her and to keep me in the loop as to what happens.

I loved Nerys. Although we hadn't kept in touch very well since I left Eastbourne we were close deep down. I looked on her as a sister, after my own sisters left. We went to school together, knocked many doors on the ministry, gave talks on the platform together, were bridesmaids at Peters wedding. I hated to see her in such an awful and dangerous situation. She deserved to be much happier.

Thinking about it later, it was just another one of those situations where the JW interpretation of scripture trumped everything else. I wondered how that kind of thing would have been dealt with back in Jesus's time. Probably the brothers of the woman would have taken the husband down a dark alley and beat seven shades of s**t out of him. Not a bad idea.

The day had flown by too quickly and before I knew it Janey was getting Bethany's shoes on and packing up their bags.

"It's been lovely seeing you, Jess," Peter said as he hugged me goodbye. "I'll be in touch about going up to see mum. You could get a train up to mine then we can drive up the rest of the way."

I couldn't help tears forming in my eyes as I hugged Bethany. I held her sleepy little face in my hands and my heart felt like it was going to actually, literally burst when she said: "Bye, Dess" and gave me a huge smile.

It had been such a good day, one that I will treasure, and when I get the photos developed they will be in frames and on my wall before the week is out. That way I can have Bethany with me all the time.

CHAPTER 15

"But what about new year celebrations? Is that against your religion too?" asked Will. Unusually, I could detect a certain amount of sarcasm. I couldn't blame him really. He'd been so patient and understanding but I think he was beginning to tire of my refusals to invitations.

"Actually, no. There's nothing directly in the Bible that says we shouldn't celebrate new beginnings but for some reason the Witnesses don't do it. I've never known them to, anyway. Maybe some of them do and it was just my mum that didn't bother." I certainly couldn't recall any event or even a mention that welcomed in the new year. New year's resolutions? What were they? Mum had once said that we should be resolved to do good things at *all* times of the year, not just at the beginning.

"So, you coming to my mate's party, then?" Will smiled encouragingly, probably hoping for a quick positive response. "He throws a great party every new year and has all the latest CDs. Be prepared for an all-nighter, Jess. You'll get no sleep, I'm telling you."

He sounded excited and I could tell he really wanted me to go. We'd done nothing together for a while now except a couple of meals out and drinks down at the harbour after work. Could I go? Should I? It would mean missing a morning out on the ministry the following day but maybe I deserved a day off.

"I'm not sure about this one, Will. Give me a bit of time to think about it, yeh? Remember the next day is a Saturday and you know what I do on Saturday mornings."

I saw his face drop. He walked away and my instinct was to call him back, give him some kind of reassurance, a glimmer of hope. But I wasn't able to. I just needed to look into this worldly activity from my adult perspective. Maybe it wouldn't be too disastrous if I were to go along.

I didn't want to keep Will waiting for my answer so the following day, after a long lie-in and a late breakfast I took a walk back up to Kathy's, knocking on the door just as they'd arrived back from an exhilarating (freezing, I would have said) morning walk. In the bookcase in the hallway I had previously spotted some bound volumes of the Watchtower and Awake magazines going back to 1972. I was sure I would find an article or two about the rights and wrongs of new year celebrations.

"Help yourself," Kathy said, "I'll put the kettle on." She left me to it and, carrying a stack of volumes into the front room, I started scanning the indexes at the back of each one. Many Witnesses kept every issue of each magazine, as mum did, but then the Society started printing each year as a nice hardback book. Easier to stand them up on the bookshelf and no more piles of tatty mags tied up with string. The only thing that the Society should have done was to choose a different colour for the covers. Kathy now had a row of 32 shit-brown volumes, a very uninviting colour which added nothing to the décor of any room. Whichever member of the Governing Body approved that colour needed to be disfellowshipped.

December 1980, the Awake. I found an article entitled: "New Year's Day – How New?" I was sure the answer would be in there. With my legs tucked under me on the sofa I began to see what they had to say.

So, the first of the many sweeping statements appeared no further in than the second paragraph: "… almost everyone drinks too much at New Year's parties." It then went on to explain that the fictional "Joe" who is contemplating going to a new year's eve party finds out that everything that he wants to do that night – "noisemaking, kissing pretty girls, drinking—descended from the rituals of ancient religions that Joe would want no part of". It discussed new year's traditions in other parts of the world, and their pagan uses of lucky charms, ways they expel demons and influence dreams.

Well, this is really boring so far and has no relevance to what happens today. It was reading like a typical Witness article, going back to the earliest reference they could possibly find in ancient texts and attaching it to the twentieth century. I scanned a few more paragraphs hoping to find something of interest and a reason valid enough to make me duck out of what I knew would be a good party.

Kathy entered the room with a mug of tea and set it down on the table next to me.

It went on to emphasise the number of alcohol-related deaths – in America, of course, as it's an American religion - and finally in the sixth section it quoted a scripture. Something about foreseeing calamity and avoiding it. Yes, wise words, I could see that.

The whole gist of the article was that drinking too much could cause you to lose control. Drink driving could kill someone or yourself. Because you are drunk you could misbehave and lose your good reputation and, finally, because you are drunk you may not be able to resist immoral temptations.

Well, this was easy in my mind: just don't get drunk.

That settled it for me. I knew I could enjoy myself without having to get totally wrecked so I decided quite quickly after reading such sound advice that there was nothing immoral about going to this party. I just had to behave myself.

Will was thrilled.

Esther was pleased too.

"It's about time you let your hair down, Jess. It's not wrong, you know. It's good you're trying to do the right thing and live a Christian life but being Christian doesn't mean you can't have any fun. Just be sensible. Stay off the spirits, yes?"

I felt almost completely comfortable about deciding to go except for the fact that I wouldn't be out on the ministry the next day. Ginny, who would be there no doubt, would be clocking my absence. She'd probably started another book on me already.

"Shopping?" suggested Will.

"Let's go." I could do with a new pair of earrings at least for a new year's eve party.

It was good to get the "silly season" over with and to finally be getting back to normal. This was the new year – 1988. The shops were open again, decorations were being taken down and packed away, and the January sales were in full swing.

I was back at work and getting ready for the first part of my training. There was a book on Mr Roade's bookshelf entitled the same as the course: "Basic Principles of Insurance." I asked if I could take it home to have a read and he thought that was a good idea. It looked pretty familiar, work that I'd already been doing, and if I could get this certificate under my belt then I could go on to sign up for the full year's course.

The only problem was that the second course was held on Thursday evenings. Yet another dilemma to get my head around. It seemed to be just one thing after another since I'd been going back to meetings. If I wasn't continually turning down invitations then it was my private life that was under scrutiny, or my choice of friends. On top of that I was still battling to have a good relationship with my mum and Peter. And now this. Oh well, I might fail at the first hurdle then the decision would be made for me.

One Sunday I was up earlier than usual and had eaten breakfast before eight. With half an hour to go to get the bus across town to the Kingdom Hall I decided to open one or two of the Christmas presents from Will's family. A fluffy jumper in shocking pink from Duncan – very sweet; a new handbag from Esther's sister Gail – I could use that for work as it's got lots of pockets and a pen holder. The present from Esther, though, brought tears to my eyes. It was such a thoughtful gift, and so beautiful. It sat in its own velvet-lined box, the excess chain tucked behind the card insert. Trust Esther to select something so personal. But looking at its glittering beauty, as the sun caught the tiny diamond in the centre, I knew I could never wear it. Jehovah's Witnesses don't wear crosses.

I remember the reasons. They insist that the Bible says Jesus died on an upright stake, not a cross. And even if it was a cross they don't made icons of things so they have nothing to do with crosses in any form. They don't even eat hot cross buns at Easter time (even if they've been reduced in Tesco's). But that could have just been mum being over the top.

How on earth was I going to break this to Esther without hurting her feelings? Could I bring myself to wear it only when she was around? No, I'd probably forget I had it on and then go to a meeting with it sitting on top of my jumper. I could imagine the looks of confusion and disgust I would get. This was yet another thing to sort out. I was hitting roadblock after roadblock and it was getting wearisome. Why couldn't life just be simple? That's all I wanted. I suppose that's what anyone wants.

I arrived at the Hall with Ginny skipping behind me. I couldn't even look at her. She disgusted me. A cliche sprang to mind: I wouldn't even spit on her if she was on fire. Such a thought was completely unchristian, but that's how I felt about this deceitful cow. Should I let her know that I found the book or leave her guessing? Most likely she will have already told the Elders about the contents, reported as many of my illicit movements as she could remember.

The chairman was on the platform waiting for everyone to settle down in their seats when one of the Elders, Brother Logan almost ran over to me and whispered:

"Can you hang around after the meeting, Jess, we just want a quick word?"

There was no time to reply as the Brother invited us to stand to sing the first song. I instantly knew what the "quick word" was about. The fact that he'd said "we" and not "I" meant it was a group of Elders that wanted to talk to me officially. Yes, it would be a little encouraging chat about my relationship status. I'd felt it coming down the trainline for weeks.

Needless to say, that was my concentration on the meeting shot to pieces. He had really picked his moment to speak to me, that Brother. I spent the whole of the first half playing out a conversation in my mind. Being questioned in turn by each of the three Elders, being asked what Will and I did with each other, who was the instigator, did we intend to get married? All those personal questions. Suddenly I was back in the little meeting room in my old congregation with those other three Elders sitting in front of me.

My adventure with Ray had been foolish but not without reason. I'd been extremely lonely and bored rigid with my Witness life. I had to change it. But it resulted in being interrogated at the age of sixteen by these "spiritual" men who wanted to know every detail of what we'd done. I attended the judicial committee meeting alone – mum couldn't cope with going so she left me to it – and the things they asked me to describe were so intrusive, I'm sure it was just for their pleasure and enjoyment. Disgusting creatures they were.

Now I could see it happening again. I was older and could probably deal with such a situation a bit better but still, they didn't have the right to grill me. By the end of the meeting I'd decided that there was actually, literally no way on this earth I would meet with any Elders ever again. I would not be put in that position under any circumstances, for any reason. And I would be more than pleased to tell them so.

After the meeting had finished I approached Brother Logan. He was quite surprised at my response. I didn't explain myself, just said, "about that chat you want, well, no, no thanks," and walked away. I felt his eyes follow me out as I headed for the foyer with a well-managed rage building up inside. Kathy was by the coat rack and, knowing me well, she could see by my face something was wrong. I just held my hand up to her, shook my head and left the Hall. If I'd had to explain there would have been tears and I'd cried too many over the years.

I'd come full circle, or so it felt. For all my efforts over the past few months I was back feeling as guilty as I did three years ago. The only way out was, as I'd rightly been told, marry Will or give him up.

"But surely if you refuse to attend a judicial meeting with them they can't take it any further? They can't ask you questions if you're not there, can they? Their interest in you will just fizzle out and they'll move on to someone else, you'll see."

Esther was just trying to help me feel better, but if she only knew how the Body of Elders in any congregation operated, how, once they got their teeth into you they would never let go, she wouldn't say such things. They were like a dog with a juicy bone and would see a judicial issue through to a satisfactory conclusion.

"Can't they see all the efforts you've made what with your meeting attendance and your regularity on the ministry? From where you were and what you've been through surely they can see how much progress you've made. But then again, I suppose they don't know about all the sacrifices you've made recently, all the things you've turned down, trying to "put the Kingdom first," as they say."

I'd used that scriptural principle in my efforts to help Will and Esther understand my stance on certain things. The phrase was easy to reel off and provided an answer to any dilemma. Blessings would follow any attempt to "put the Kingdom first" so no-one would lose out, not really.

"Do you want me to have a word with them, Jess, put them in the picture? If they had a better understanding of your circumstances, about your past experiences and the difficulties you're still facing with your mum, I'm sure they'd be more sympathetic."

"Ah, Esther, thank you, but there's no room for sympathy in the Truth. Rules are rules and they're made to be enforced as far as the Elders are concerned. They exist to keep the congregation clean from the likes of fornicators like me! But, actually," I suddenly had a lightbulb moment, "yes, you're right. If I didn't actually attend the meeting they'd have nothing to go on, would they?"

For a moment, I had the tiniest glimmer of hope that I wouldn't be forced to make a decision.

"I suppose my dear friend Ginny has clued them up on my whereabouts and how many times Will has stayed here overnight, but really that's her word against mine. She's just putting two and two together and making a meal of whatever she's seen. If I actually attended the judicial I could deny it all." I felt a little excitement well up. "That would really make her look a fool."

"It's something to think about."

I'd been away from the Organisation for three years. Maybe the rules had changed. Perhaps there was a way through this without losing everything all over again.

That evening Peter called. It was good to hear his voice and we had a relaxed chat and a bit of a laugh at Charlie's receding hairline. Then it was down to business. We set a date for me to get the train up to Victoria. Peter would meet me there and we'd drive the rest of the way up to mum's. It should take about two hours. Stay overnight at mum's then head back the next day. We agreed on Saturday 6th February and hung up after wishing each other well.

"...and give Bethany big hugs and kisses from me, won't you?"

I'd enlarged one of the photos I'd taken of Bethany when they were down on boxing day. The ten-by-eight-inch framed shot of her looking straight at the camera stood next to the mirror on my dressing table. Her eyes had caught the flash and were tinged with red – I didn't have Will's technical skills to avoid such things. But she looked beautiful. Her cheeks were flushed as we'd not long returned from the park and the dolly she held in her hand was just about wearing two pairs of shoes, having been squeezed into place. Bethany had a thing about shoes, it seemed. The weekend I would see her, I'd take her shopping for some new footwear, let her choose them herself. I bet she'd love that.

I put the entry in my diary and would tell Will I'd be away that weekend. He'd have plenty to occupy him. That was a good thing about our relationship: although we were very close, we didn't suffocate each other. Will had his space and I had mine and it worked well. We trusted each other completely. Even without this "get married or else" dagger hanging over our heads I don't think either of us felt any need to tie the knot. I certainly didn't, and I wouldn't be pushed into it by anyone.

Devouring that book on the Basic Principles of Insurance was worth the effort. I passed the one-day course and received my shiny certificate which Mr Roades asked me to display on the office wall. I felt so chuffed with myself for achieving something. I almost rang mum to tell her, but I just knew there would be no hint of excitement or pride in her voice and I didn't want to hear her dull tones. Mum's view of achieving anything in this world was that it was simply a waste of time because the end of this wicked system of things is just around the corner. I wished she could just be proud of me for once and make the effort to show it. It would mean such a lot.

Mr Roades set up a start date with the college for Thursday 25th February. Class started at 7pm and lasted till 9. It couldn't have been scheduled at a worse time. I still didn't know what I was going to do. This was something I just couldn't deal with. I couldn't justify missing every Thursday meeting for a year. There would be questions, accusations about putting education before Kingdom interests. And how could I possibly explain to Mr Roades that I wouldn't be able to attend the course? Each time the problem arose in my head I put it to the back of the queue, but I knew that at some point I'd have to deal with it.

The cold was really setting in now. Snow didn't often settle in this area, not with the salty sea air, but we had a couple of inches overnight which froze. Esther's car was sparkly in the morning sunlight as she stood scraping the ice off the windscreen, wrapped up in her thick woolly scarf and furry hat. I watched her from the kitchen as I drank my tea. So dependable, reliable and at the same time flexible, willing to give anything a go. That was my Esther. I was scared to think what my life would be like now if I hadn't met her and Will.

She came back in the front door to fill the bucket with lukewarm water, blowing her nose as she did.

"That's some thick ice today, it's not shifting at all," she snuffled, her nose red and sore-looking.

"Want some help, Esther?"

"No, love, you get ready for work, I'll just keep at it."

As I left the house, I heard her coughing and blowing her nose. I'd never known Esther to be ill. She was as fit as a fiddle, always the one to look after others.

By Thursday, Esther's cold had turned into something nasty and that morning she asked me to ring the doctor when I got to work. Surgery didn't open til 9 so I rang just after. The doctor made a house call and when I called Esther back at lunchtime she told me he thought it was a chest infection.

"I used to have them every winter but none for a few years now," she wheezed down the line.

I insisted she get tucked up in bed, and when I got home I made her some soup. She had a TV in her room, such a luxury, and the six o'clock news theme tune played as I sat at her dressing table and dipped the corner of a slice of bread in my bowl of oxtail.

"Shouldn't you be getting ready for your meeting, Jess?" her raspy voice only just reaching above the TV noise.

"I'm staying here tonight. Not going to leave you when you're like this. I'll fetch the Radio Times so you can see what's on the box tonight."

She rested and read and watched TV and swallowed her cough mixture throughout the evening and I took care of her as best I could. There's a fine line between taking care of someone and making too much fuss, and I hoped Esther would tell me if I was overdoing it with the bedside manner. When I looked in on her at about ten o'clock she'd laid down and I could see the rise and fall of the bedclothes as she breathed her way into a deep sleep. I gently pulled the door to and took myself off to bed. The doctor said he would prepare a prescription for antibiotics to be collected in the morning. Mr Roades wouldn't mind me being a bit late into work once I'd explained, I was sure.

Poor ol' Esther. It took her a while to recover and she hated taking time off work. Usually she could swap shifts with another nurse but it wasn't always possible. Her symptoms eased after about a week and I saw her energy slowly return.

Sunday came round. I'd found a nice jumper in the C & A sale. A soft pink, lacy with a section around the neck that was beaded. I went well with my navy skirt and I felt good in it. It ticked all the boxes: no low neckline, not too tight, not distracting in anyway. Kathy would admire it, I knew she would. She'd been trying out inserting beads into her crocheted squares recently. Kathy always had some new craft underway.

The bus was late. I hated being late for anything. I'd rather be early and have to kill some time than rush around finding a seat, apologising for disturbing the row of settled families as I barged through. At least I managed to get there just at the end of the opening prayer and not right in the middle. I took my seat and looked ahead. I was right behind

Ginny. Great. I'd have the back of her head to stare at for the next two hours.

The public talk was something about who we can put our trust in during these fearful last days. I was struggling to concentrate as it was my time of the month and this one was more painful than usual. I was experiencing pain with not actually that much to show for it and I wished I'd taken a couple of Disprin before I left the house. My pad didn't feel that securely positioned which added to the problem. My arms across my middle provided a bit of warmth and comfort but I still wasn't relaxed enough to fully tune in to the speaker.

About twenty minutes into the talk the family to my left suddenly started shuffling around, putting their books back in their bags. They left and, not wanting to turn round in my seat, I presumed they'd gone home for some reason. Oh well, that meant I could spread out a bit, use the seat next to me as a table for my books.

My mind drifted to the beach, the salty crust that formed on my skin after a dip, and I realised I couldn't wait for spring to start swimming again. Cold water swimming? Yeh, I'd give it a go. I'd just wrap up really warm when I got out and get back to the house as quick as I could. Tomorrow. Tomorrow I'll do it, take an icy plunge and a hot chocolate to follow.

The second half of the meeting was as difficult as the first and I was relieved to hear the chairman announce the final song, "Let's sing a song of praise to Jehovah, Brothers and Sisters. Song 92." I stood up, carefully, smoothing my skirt down at the back.

I thought I'd give Ginny a treat by singing louder than normal, right in her ear. I saw her flinching but I carried on. I secretly wished there was something else I could do to make her realise how much she'd hurt me and the answer soon came, quite unplanned, but absolutely perfect.

All eyes were closed. The silence that was only present during a prayer was deafening as everyone listened to the words of thanks and praise from the visiting speaker. It was a time for absolute stillness. As I stood there the discomfort I had been feeling with my pad suddenly resolved itself as the thing came completely unstuck and made its way out flopping onto the floor between my legs. I didn't know what to do. I kicked it around, trying to move it under my bag, put my foot on it. Thank goodness everyone had their eyes closed! Such a wicked thought went through my mind as I spied Ginny's bag gaping open on the seat next to her. Yes. This was my chance. *Thanks, Ginny. I'll always remember you for saving me from a very embarrassing moment.*

I let out a sigh and a very satisfied snort as I sat on the toilet and sorted myself out straight after the prayer was over. Now, before I leave, who did I need to speak to today? Kathy, about that ministry bag she had for me, a couple of Sisters from my group to arrange who to work with on the ministry next Saturday, oh, and I needed to collect my magazines from the literature desk. I sought out Kathy who was deep in conversation with an Elder. They both looked at me as I approached, then carried on talking. Hmm.

I guess it wasn't appropriate to interrupt them right now. I'll catch her later.

At the back of the Hall by the sound desk I spotted the family that had been sitting next to me. I thought they'd left but they must have just changed seats. A bit odd. I headed over to the mother, Anne.

"Hi, Anne, how's things? Are you going out on Saturday?" I tried to meet her eyes but she quickly turned away.

"Anne? Is everything all right?" I pushed.

Before I'd finished the question she'd scuttled off. I turned to her daughter.

"Clare, is your mum ok? Is she unwell?"

Clare too turned around and made her way out towards the foyer.

What was going on? From the furthest point at the back of the Hall I could see Kathy looking directly at me. I held my shoulders up and hands out in a questioning pose but Kathy, too, turned away.

Then it dawned on me. Oh, I get it. I get the game they're playing. They've all decided to give me the cold shoulder to make me come to my senses. There must have been an announcement on Thursday that I've been "marked". I'm officially bad association, someone to be avoided from now on, due to my loose morals. Well, thank a lot, Elders. That has really cheered me up. Just because I refused to let you "have a word" with me. Everyone avoiding me is really going to help me with my "loose morals." Not this again. Not this big arrow above my head pointing down to the bad example.

Bag in hand, I marched over to Brother Logan and demanded to know what had been going on.

"You've announced that I've been marked, haven't you?" I didn't wait for his answer. "When was it announced? Last Thursday? Why? And why didn't you at least tell me? That would have been a decent thing to do."

He took me to one side, out of earshot of others hanging around.

"We had to do it, Jess. You gave us no choice. But, no, you haven't been marked. We had a meeting to discuss your situation and, given that you refused to speak to us, we took the only course of action open to us.........."

I knew what was coming. My death sentence. A complete cutting off with the sharpest blade they could find: "………which was to disfellowship you."

CHAPTER 16

A noise like wild rushing water filled my head, it swished around and all sound from other sources had stopped. The next thing I knew I was sitting on a chair with a glass of water in my hand and Brother Dolan crouched down at my side. My heart was beating out of my chest and I was desperately trying to control my breathing, not wanting to go into full panic mode, my usual reaction to sudden stress. I squeezed the glass.

Dolan's words came at me as if through mud, "I'm sorry Jess. For what it's worth, I voted against the decision but I was out-voted. I know you'll sort yourself out in time but right now we need to protect the congregation. You'll make your way back, I know you will, you've done it before."

I raised my head and looked him straight in the eye. I couldn't believe what I was hearing. Is this some kind of nightmare? The ringing in my ears was not going anywhere. I could barely hear my own voice as I tried to respond to his revelation:

"You f…. You f…." I couldn't get the word out. Was something preventing me from swearing in God's house or had my power of speech simply left me?

There was no point arguing, appealing the decision, no benefit in discussing it. The deed was done and couldn't be undone. They had killed me – again.

I could faintly hear the traffic, a car tooting its horn, a cyclist swerving around me and shouting some obscenity. It had started to rain, a misty, dewy rain, the kind that soaks you to the skin. A tiny break in the clouds revealed a bright blue January sky and the wind was pushing to cover it up again.

I wasn't cold. No coat or scarf or hat. I'd left them all behind. My bag was all I needed, though now I'd arrived at my destination it was much lighter than before. Someone would find the discarded songbook in the large puddle beneath the football goal; the Watchtower torn into quarters and scattered to the wind along Grove Road. My Silvine notepad half full of scriptures from talks gone by I'd dropped in a bin somewhere.

I lay there looking up into the sky. The softness of the grass beneath me was comforting beyond belief and in that quiet moment I thought what a simple thing grass really was, and yet so pleasing. A blanket for the earth, downy hair on a new baby's back, a canvas to build upon. Beneath the grass the solid hills supported me. They weren't going anywhere. Been there since the beginning of time.

Brother Dolan's words came back to me: "You'll make your way back, I know you will, you've done it before."

No. My life is over. There's no point to it anymore. Discarded like a single glove. I've lost my family, again. They've stolen them from me, again.

I'll never see them or speak to them again. Bethany will grow up not knowing me. I'm certainly not good enough to be part of God's family, I can see that now. If I haven't got Jehovah's favour then I will die when Armageddon comes along with the all other non-Witnesses. Why should I wait for that to happen? I could save myself from a lot of heartache.

I rolled over onto my front and wriggled further towards the edge. This cliff will hold me up while I hang my head over the edge and watch the seagulls making circles in the crisp air. Some chalk crumbled under my hands and I followed its path as far as was visible down the six hundred feet to the rocks below. I could see the waves down there, crashing into the jagged edges of the huge flint and chalk masses. Sucked away only to crash again and again and again in a never-ending cycle. The tide doesn't stop, the waves crash, the earth turns, the sun rises and sets. It rains. These things are certainties when nothing else is. Everything else changes. It stops, ends, switches direction, catches me out, trips me up, throws me away.

On my back again I searched for that piece of blue sky. It had disappeared, covered over by grey clouds full of darkness and misery. Unreleased tears now set themselves free and ran down the sides of my face. I let them come. Freely and noisily.

My foot was being pushed from side to side, the dog panting and sniffing and nudging. It sat down next to me and I turned my head till our eyes met. It just sat there, looking at me and it seemed like forever. The owner called and still it stayed. A second, louder, firmer call took it away and I heard it scampering off, imagining the thundering of its feet reverberating right into the depths of the cliffs.

Time stood still. The sun stayed hidden. It rained. I rested, numb to the world.

When I woke it was getting dark. I was on my side and could feel the weight of a blanket over me. Strong hands lifted me and I felt myself being transported onto a wheeled bed. I kept my eyes closed as I was bumped along the grass away from the edge of the earth.

Charlie had a kind face. When he smiled at me I couldn't help but smile back. But that simple smile produced a surge of emotion and fat tears followed soon after. The chaplain at Beachy Head held my hand gently but firmly as the ambulance rolled along. He pushed strands of wet hair back off my face. He spoke now and again, softly, pointing out that his role as Charlie the chaplain had raised a few smiles over the years. I gave a small laugh, then cried again.

"Just let it all out, there's a girl. No point keeping it all locked up inside." His soft voice was low and soothing and I wanted to sleep again. I had no energy.

"We're nearly there now, just round the corner and we'll get you checked over."

"Sharp scratch......Fluids....temperature a bit high........." I heard mumblings in the distance, women's voices, men's, giving instructions, shoes squeaking across the floor, curtains swishing open and closed. Blurred faces stared at me in between stretches of silence.

I had no idea of the time or even what day it was. Cocooned in this curtained bay there was no view of any windows so see if it was light or dark outside. I took a deep breath and attempted to sit up in the bed. Oh man! Did my body ache. I felt like I'd been run over by a bus. I pulled the thin sheet up under my neck as shivers ran through my body every few seconds. A chill had certainly taken hold, not surprising really as I must have been soaked through with all that rain. The curtain was drawn back and a nurse popped her head in.

"Jessica, how are you feeling?" She took a long look at me and inspected the monitors I was hooked up to. I felt the cuff on my arm tighten as my blood pressure was recorded again.

"That's fine," she said, sliding the loosened cuff down my arm. "Ready for a cup of tea and some toast?"

"Yes, please." My throat felt dry and a cuppa would be very welcome.

"We've rung someone in your address book called Esther and she's just arrived. Do you want to see her now?"

Oh, god, Esther. Did I want to see her? Yes, of course I did, but I didn't want to explain anything. I couldn't face going through it all just yet. I nodded to the nurse.

Seeing Esther's lovely face produced another bout of tears and sobs. She held me without words, hugged me and stroked my head. We stayed like that for what seemed ages. I felt so safe and so loved and so warm. She didn't let go till my sobbing settled down and my grip on her relaxed. I owed her something, though. She must have been worried when I didn't arrive home at my usual time after a Sunday meeting.

"They did it, Esther," I whispered, "I've been disfellowshipped again. And nobody bothered to tell me." I hung my head, unable to look at her. I didn't want to see my own anger reflected in her face. She would understand immediately what being disfellowshipped meant. The public announcement, the instruction to the congregation not to talk to me. She got it.

"Right." I could hear her rage in that single word. She would be prepared to march straight round to Dolan's house and give him what for, I knew she would. She slapped her hands on her knees and stood up sharply.

"I'm so glad you're safe, Jess. Let's get you home, shall we?"

Intuitive as always, she knew I didn't want to elaborate. Her priority was to take care of me right now, and I loved her for it.

CHAPTER 17

Will tightened his arms around me as we lay on the bed. He was quiet, just let me be. I sensed, though, he didn't know quite what to say, so he said nothing. Maybe he was waiting to gauge how I was in case he came out with the wrong thing. A gentle, kind man. Should I have accepted his proposal of marriage so this situation could be avoided? No. I had no regrets on that score. No one was going to push me into any decision whatever the consequences would be.

Mum, Peter. How do I tell them? I guess by now, though, that Kathy would have been on the phone to both of them. Well, let her. That makes it easier for me. I wouldn't need to hear the disappointment in their voices, their unspoken 'I told you so's.

Again, Dolan's words came to me: "You'll make your way back, I know you will, you've done it before." He didn't know what he was talking about. He made it sound as simple as eating a burger in the Wimpy. Get up, go to the loo, come back and carry on from where you left off. But it's not the same. You have to jump through hoops to be reinstated, be the perfect Witness, with perfect meeting attendance whilst at the same time carrying bucket loads of shame and embarrassment round your neck. Every meeting sitting on the back row as instructed, deemed too diseased and infectious to be allowed to sit anywhere else. That's all they can judge you on – meeting attendance. There is no discussion, no interaction with the Elders whatsoever so they don't know how difficult it is to get there every Sunday and Thursday. So, they watch and they record and they wait, while you listen to the voices of former friends talking through the microphone about showing Christian love whilst trying to square that with how they are treating you right now. Something just doesn't add up. No hellos, no goodbyes. No support. Alone. For months and months without knowing if or when it will end. When you make an application for reinstatement and then, following a meeting with the Elders, wait and wait again with no indication as to the outcome. Then one evening you unexpectedly hear your name from the platform, it grabs your waning attention and you hear "……..has been reinstated into the Christian congregation." There's no reaction from the congregation until after the meeting is over. Hugs and kisses, as though they've truly missed you. Maybe some of them have. Others walk past and will still never speak. The damage is done and you will never be allowed to forget it.

No. I can't do it. Not again. Not even for mum, Peter, Bethany. Oh, my Bethany! My darling niece! I will miss you so much. The upcoming trip to see mum with Peter won't happen now. There won't be any trips to the shops with Bethany to get new shoes. My tears flowed again, nose all snotty on the pillow.

Will reached behind him and passed me a tissue. He stroked my arm.

This is not right. How can it be a Christian thing to do? And those Elders didn't even have the decency to tell me they were going to announce it. So, they don't want me in their club. "Living in sin," they used to call it. Well, ok, myself and half the world are living in sin and so did Adam and Eve. They didn't get married. Didn't have a ceremony to announce their union. God just put them together and told them not to have it off with anyone else. Will is the only man for me, we're loyal and faithful to each other and all our true friends know it. So, what's the problem?

I suppose the expectation to marry developed over centuries. Traditions, rituals, habits. That's the way it's always been. Which is laughable: the Witnesses were so keen to point out that they have nothing to do with "this wicked world" that we live in and yet they allowed themselves to get sucked into all their traditions – well, some of them. The ones that suit them. They were a joke. And I'd been made a laughing stock.

A million thoughts were whizzing through my brain, starting down one path then doubling back – mum's opinion, Peter's viewpoint, the Elders, the congregation, Kathy. I swung from giving them all excuses to feeling such bitterness and anger and dread. I knew how they were going to treat me, I could feel that hurt all over again – it had ripped open my heart and embedded itself in the deepest part, squeezing harder with each meeting I attended, with the sight of every Witness that passed me by on the street, not speaking when before, we would have hugged.

I couldn't take all that again. I needed to talk it all through, somehow. But who could possibly understand? I mean *really* understand. Esther and Will were great sounding boards but I needed help to make sense of it, to help me to, I don't know, see things in a different way perhaps. In a way that wasn't going to lead me to self-destruction. It could so easily. I could bury my head in this pillow and not get up again. I could drink myself to death, start taking drugs, throw myself under the train that runs on the track behind the Kingdom Hall – now that would be ironic. I could have stepped off the edge yesterday. Into oblivion. Into the end. But for some reason I didn't.

Monday morning, and I felt Will stirring early. The clock said seven and daylight framed the peachy flowered curtains. He knew I was awake and whispered that he was going to hang around here today instead of going to work. He was a good man.

Even before I got out of bed I knew my legs would be wobbly. A cough had developed overnight but despite feeling so rough I wanted to move about. Downstairs, Esther was sitting at the table, pen in hand.

"Hi, love, how are you feeling? She gave me a sympathetic look. "Hungry?"

"Not really. I feel so dirty though, could do with a bath." I sat down and pulled my dressing gown around my cold legs, covering my mouth as another cough emerged. "Who are you writing to?" Her writing set was spread out on the table, a picture of a lavender field on the case just visible under the stack of envelopes.

"I'm writing to your mum."

"Oh, no Esther. Please. It's not her fault, any of this."

"Don't worry, I'm not going to have a go at your mum. You've explained well enough the ins and outs of this disfellowshipping practice, and I feel I have a good understanding of it. I Just want to point out a few things, you know, mother to mother. Time passes by so quickly and maybe she needs to think about things long term. I'll be gentle." She put her hand on mine and gave it a squeeze.

"Well, if you think it'll do any good. I won't hold my breath for a phone call from her, though." There was nothing to lose by Esther writing to mum. Actually, literally nothing at all. I'd lost it all already.

Esther made me a cup of tea and some toast while I stroked Petra. I'd let her sleep on the bed between us, which was a first. Now, she sat at my feet looking up at me and occasionally laying her head on my knee.

As I blew on my tea Esther slid a leaflet across the table towards me. "Help is Out There" it read, and the picture of a beautiful landscape spread across both front and the back. It was from the Chaplaincy service and there was a phone number inside. Their words were encouraging:

"Braced: we are ready and equipped to help anyone in need.

Hopeful: we believe that positive change is always possible.

Compassionate: we show care towards everyone, no matter who they are.

Tireless: we are ready to respond every hour of every day, and we never give up on people."

They stated that never give up on people. Well, that's different to what I've just experienced.

I knew that they were involved in the church somehow and, despite my ingrained belief that all other religions were evil, I wondered if there would be someone that I could talk to. I had to put aside all of my automatic responses and start thinking about the bigger picture. Their service used other organisations including mental health professionals and counsellors which might be useful. Seeing a worldly counsellor was highly discouraged amongst the Witnesses but I was not interested in any of their rules now. Maybe a Christian counsellor would be able to see things from a spiritual standpoint.

My fear was that I would be told that I had only got what I deserved, that the actions of the Elders were actually correct. But I can't imagine that all other Christian religions did this disfellowshipping thing. There would be riots, protests, court cases. No, it had to be wrong. I resolved to dial the number later on after work. Work!!!!

"Esther, I'm supposed to be at work!" I almost shouted, a panic setting in.

"Calm down, Jess. I phoned you in sick for the next three days. Didn't give Mr Roades any details, just said you were dealing with a crisis at the moment."

"Oh, Esther, you think of everything. Thank you." Her actions set me off crying again and I hugged her, kissing the top of her head. I relaxed and finished my tea and toast, took a couple of Disprin and ruffled Petra's soft ears.

"I think I'll have that bath, now," I announced, standing up to go.

"Can I ask you something, Jess, before you go? You said that last time this happened you managed to keep your faith. That you didn't blame God, but the Elders' interpretation of certain scriptures. Do you think that's the case this time?"

I wrapped my arms around myself. This was something I needed to think about. Perhaps I needed to see those scriptures for myself. Do a bit of research. Look for clear evidence either way. But then, if Bible scholars who had studied those texts for years and years, as the founders of the religion had done, had come up with this interpretation, then who was I to say they'd got it wrong?

"Not sure, Esther. Not sure."

Following my bath, I dialled the number on the leaflet. Charlie the Chaplain answered. After quite a long conversation I made an appointment for the following day. They used an office in town and Will said he'd take me, go off and do some bits at the shops and bring me back. I needed to be occupied today, though, keep my mind on positive things and Will knew just what would do the trick. We spent the day looking through his old family photo albums. Snaps from the sixties and seventies, in black and white and colour, square and rectangular, with crumpled edges and drying glue behind the clear film on each page. His flares and platforms gave us the biggest laughs not to mention his hair. Long black curls touched his shoulders and, being so tall, his short brown tank top didn't quite reach the top of his trousers. At least he could laugh at himself. We moved on to pictures of his dad who had passed away suddenly when Will was just eight years old. I guess all of us have to learn to live with things we'd rather not. Will didn't have a choice back then either. He had to get on with it, and he survived despite how devastated he must have felt.

After lunch we took Petra for a short walk round the block. I didn't want to stay out too long, not with my cough and cold.

Will busied himself with some paperwork he'd brought with him and I got a pen and writing pad out of the drawer with the intention of writing to mum. My thoughts formed the first line: "Dear mum, by now you would have heard that I've been disfellowshipped," but beyond that I could get no further. The words wouldn't come. There was no point in trying to explain my relationship with Will, she would take the moral high ground and my ink would be wasted. There was no hope of her replying. I pushed the pen and paper away and followed it with a deep sigh.

The following day I walked through the door bearing the notice 'Beachy Head Chaplaincy Service'. Charlie was seated in the cosy room equipped with a box of tissues on the low table. He introduced me to Patricia, an older lady with flowing skirts and smelling of patchouli. She reminded me of Kathy a bit. They made me feel very welcome and we talked for a couple of hours. Well, I talked, they listened for the first hour, then I sat back and heard a side that I'd never considered before. Patricia admitted she had never come across a situation quite like this before and she couldn't see how this treatment would entice anyone to go back, not for the right reasons anyway. After asking a series of searching questions, she made a few suggestions that really made me think. She gave me comfort, assured me that I had been treated unfairly and, no, this definitely was not the done thing within other churches, except there was something similar within the Mormons. There was confession and forgiveness – probably the same amount of gossip – but on the whole members were welcomed whatever their status. But the best thing about the discussion was that she gave me hope.

Later on that evening, comfortably seated in the front room with coffee in hand, I recounted to Esther some of what we'd discussed.

"One thing Patricia made clear right from the start is that it's not *my* choice not to speak to them. "Let's get this straight," she said, "is it you that's banned from talking to them?" "No," I said, "it's they who are told not to talk to me."" It's *their* decision, Esther. They are the ones that choose to follow the Elders' instructions to ostracise me. I can go and talk to them if I please, can't I? I know I won't get any response but, hey, it would make them feel uncomfortable, wouldn't it? I'm not the one that's trapped. They are. She managed to turn the whole thing round and what she said made so much sense." I'd come to that conclusion myself before but for some reason, to hear it confirmed from someone else made it real. It wasn't simply my own wishful musings.

Esther just let me ramble on, nodding in agreement: "it's not written in British Law, any of this. It's not illegal for them to talk to me. They're not going to get arrested if they get caught saying hi to me, they won't be thrown in prison. Big Brother is not watching them. No, they choose to do it of their own free will."

"But I remember you saying that if someone carries on talking to a disfellowshipped person, they're in line for the same treatment. It would look like they're condoning that person's so-called immoral life and then they'll be cast out as well."

"That's right. BUT, do you know something? I have *never* heard of that happening. Not once. I've never even heard of anyone who has known that to happen. They live in fear of being caught out, being seen and reported to the Elders. I suppose some of them might genuinely believe I'm being thoroughly immoral, I don't know."

Esther was listening intently and taking me seriously. Petra joined the conversation by plodding over and leaning her head on my knee.

"So….. Kathy, Greg, Ginny….well, let's forget about that bitch…. Mum, Peter, they are all going to choose to give up their relationships with me for what could be the rest of my life based on what the

Elders tell them to do. The stupid thing is, even if I were to put things right in their eyes by getting married to Will, that wouldn't change anything, because I'd still be disfellowshipped."

"This is crazy, Jess. And where do you think your mum stands on all of this?" a reasonable question which, after a moment's thought, I attempted to answer.

"I suppose mum is of that generation that was brought up to believe it was a sin and, given that she was raised an Irish Catholic, the threat of burning in Hell forever would have made its mark on her too. Peter, though, hmmm, not sure about him. He's a devout Witness but I'd like to think some part of his brain is not totally controlled by the Elders. I suppose what I'm trying to say is that in some weird way I hope he's going to find this as hard as I am."

She shook her head, put her feet up on the footstool and readjusted the cushion behind her back. "What else did Patricia have to say? You said she gave you hope."

"Yes, with regards to Bethany. She said to keep in mind that one day Bethany will make up her own mind about me. Time will pass and soon enough she'll be a stroppy teenager, headstrong and wanting to go her own way. So, I should write her letters. There's a chance that she might get to read them, maybe not all of them, but hopefully some, and she'll grow up knowing who I am."

"Good idea."

"Although my biggest fear about Bethany is that she'll be thoroughly indoctrinated like I was. That poor girl. My heart aches for her already, Esther, when I think about all the things she's going to miss out on while growing up – parties, dancing, after-school clubs, school trips, building friendships with normal people."

"But there's nothing you can do about that, Jess. All you can do is be there for her when she's ready to find you. In the meantime, why not spend a bit more time with Charlotte and Spencer? They love you, I'm sure they'd be pleased to go out for the day with you, bring them here to the beach, make a campfire. They'd love it and it would help Annabel too."

That was such a good idea. I needed to write down my plan of action, my survival guide. If I was going to get through this – not even get through it, as there didn't appear to be an end in sight – but learn to live with this situation, then I needed to be focussed on positive things, look ahead instead of behind and make use of the good things I had in my life. In short, I needed to count my blessings.

CHAPTER 18

One of my biggest blessings was my job. The first day I went back was a bit difficult as my cold was getting me down and I still felt a bit wobbly, but I managed to get through the day without making too many mistakes. Work was a good distraction and my colleagues just got on with their tasks and didn't ask any questions. As far as they knew I'd been off due to a nasty cold. It was only Mr Roades who Esther had mentioned a 'crisis' to. But none of them were aware of how drastically my life had changed overnight, how it would never be the same again. Waiting for the kettle to boil for the seventh time that day my mind kept slinking off to mum and Peter. Had Kathy been on the phone to them yet? She wasn't a gossipy type but for something as important as this I don't think she would have delayed in passing on the news.

Saturday afternoon I made myself go out for a brisk walk with Petra along the beach. Wrapping myself up warm we headed towards the Aqua Bar, Petra running ahead as usual. The fresh air did me good as I filled my lungs and watched the gulls circling above. It was a chilly but bright day and the receding tide was calling me. I wondered again if I could be brave enough to go for a cold swim. Perhaps in a few more weeks, we'd be into March by then.

By the time we got back I felt well and truly done in and just wanted to sit quietly in front of the telly. Will had arrived while I was out and gave me such a big hug once I'd shed my coat, hat, scarf, gloves, pink ear-muffs, and woolly leg warmers. We sat in the lounge and had a cuddle and a catch up on the last few days. I assured him of my resolutions, the encouragement I'd got from Patricia and the ideas she'd put forward. Will said he'd be keeping a close eye on me to make sure I carried out my plan of writing to Bethany.

"In fact, why don't you write the first letter now? It doesn't need to be too long."

"Oh, not right now, Will, I need to think about what to say. I'll do it tomorrow. Ok? I suppose I'd better write to mum as well, it's only decent to tell her myself."

"You will cope with this, Jess. As hard as it seems right now, you're a survivor and there will be better times ahead with your family, I'm sure. Hey, Peter might even run off and have an affair or take up gambling or smoking and get disfellowshipped himself! Anything's possible."

I doubted anything like that would ever happen.

"I'm going to miss mum's wedding. I don't even know when it is."

"Surely she'd tell you, something as important as a wedding?"

"Probably not. I've heard of people having died and their disfellowshipped relative wasn't even told. They had no chance to say goodbye or even attend the funeral. It's disgusting behaviour."

Esther popped her head into the room and announced she'd got a few friends coming round in a bit and would I give her a hand in the kitchen. I took the tray of sausage rolls out of the oven and set about quartering up a dozen scotch eggs and squirting the dressing on the salad. A sharp knock on the door made me jump, sloshing the orange squash out of the jug. Two familiar voices made me stop mopping up, voices I hadn't heard in a little while. Charlotte and Spencer skipped towards me with their arms outstretched. It was so good to see them, and more hugs with Theresa and Neil made me almost tearful.

"What are you doing here!?"

Before they could answer there was another knock and in walked Sandy and Ellie, each carrying a six-pack and huge bag of crisps.

"What's going on Esther?" She was up to something.

"Thought you could do with some time with your friends, your true friends, Jess. Dominic should be here soon and some others you know."

I didn't know what to say. This was exactly what I needed right now. To be in the company of people who liked me for who I was, for just being me. It was reassuring that I still mattered in this world, that I wasn't the lowest of the low in most people's eyes.

We spent the evening playing games with the kids, eating and drinking and playing music. Ellie had brought along a mini disco ball and hung it from the light fitting in the front room. Someone pushed the coffee table back and we had our own little disco. The kids loved it. Everyone loved it.

"So, Dixieland next Saturday then?" suggested Sandy. "It's been a long time. Dig your gear out and get your hair dyed again, let's do this thing!" she sang, bobbing away with a can in her hand to the beat of a Communards hit. Charlotte was dancing with Will, two-handed, with twirls and side steps. Spencer was licking the empty crisp bowl. Theresa and Neil were doing their own thing in between flicking through the records, lining up the next tracks to play. Esther's sister and some of her friends arrived at the same time as Dominic. He seemed to have got over his issue with my rejection all those months ago and was completely fine with me now. The chatter level increased, the volume of the music went up and it was such a joy to be with these people, see them relaxed in their own skin. They made me feel as if I could truly be just me.

My letter to mum was the hardest I'd ever written to anyone. I made it short and to the point, asking her directly when she was getting married. I didn't apologise for my behaviour, for living in sin, as I kept in mind my own conclusions I'd come to on the subject of marriage or rather, weddings. One thing I did include, though, was a question. I really hoped that one day she would do me the favour of telling me why, all those years ago, she chose to become one of Jehovah's Witnesses. Why that religion above all others. I mean, she'd told me that she'd been searching for something meaningful in her life back in the late sixties and having tried Buddhism and the Methodists and several other religions she'd settled on the Witnesses. I could really do with knowing why. I left it at that after telling her that I will miss her and that I love her very much. Yes, I cried.

Several weeks passed and March was drawing to a close and I still hadn't managed to get myself in the sea. The weather had been mixed with cold but bright sunny days so I'd had no excuse really, just hadn't got round to it. I'd settled into my insurance course, having no reason not to do it, now that my Thursday nights were free. At least that was one good thing about all this. I really threw myself into my studies and did extra work between each session. What I was learning at college came in useful at work and Mr Roades introduced me to a different set of tasks. I could put into practice what I was learning and it made me feel valued in the business, that I was part of a growing project and had an important part to play in its success.

I had become a regular babysitter for Theresa and Neil as the kids were still staying with them every now and then. Theresa was happy to tell me that Annabel was making progress with her counselling and seemed to be coping a bit better with life. I'm sure the spring sunshine helped her state of mind too. The tiny buds on the leaves and the daffodil bulbs pushing through the soil. I hope Annabel noticed those things and was able to take pleasure in them. There seemed to be something comforting in the reliability of nature – knowing that no matter how uncertain life could be at times, the seasons would always come round, flowers would grow and the sun would shine.

They'd been able to go out for a nice romantic anniversary meal while I played Connect Four with Charlotte. Spencer joined in but his attention span only lasted long enough to drop two discs into random slots. At the instructed time I settled them in bed and, after the ten o'clock news, took myself off to the spare room. It was easier for me to stay overnight and get a lift back home in the morning. It was like being part of a family and I loved it. I still thought about my family from time to time, especially my three sisters, and wondered how their lives were panning out. I began to view Theresa as a sister and the bond between us was growing as time passed.

The weekend arrived and Will suggested a few drinks down at the Castle Inn. We hadn't really been out that much together lately, not feeling up to clubbing, myself. Ah, the Castle Inn. A popular pub. Old, with low beamed ceilings and latches on the door. It had been ages since we'd been in here. I chose a table while Will went to order at the bar. Cinzano and lemonade for me, nothing too heavy. There was some low, barely audible music playing and after a couple of drinks I felt like asking the barman to turn it up.

"There's the old Jess, there she is," remarked Will as I tapped a drum beat on the table. "Looks like you might be ready to get back down to Dixieland soon, then." Maybe it was time to get myself up on that dance floor again.

The bells over the door jangled as it opened, bringing in a gust of wind and an empty crisp packet someone had discarded outside. My face dropped as I saw who it was. That bitch and her smarmy-looking husband. My hand tightened on Will's leg. They hadn't spotted us yet. There weren't many Witnesses that lived out in Pevensey Bay so I hadn't really bumped into anyone since I'd been dumped. But now here I was face to face with the one who'd had it in for me from very early on. The one who'd followed me, spied on me, pretended to be friends with me, had made a detailed record of all my encounters with Will.

I hoped my used sanitary towel had not made too much of a mess in her bag. I'd shoved it down as far as it would go so she wouldn't find it till the next meeting - actually, literally squashed between her Bible and newly printed magazines. Well, she deserved it.

Geoff was at the bar, his foot resting on the brass rail at foot level, and Ginny had found a couple of spare seats at a table near the fireplace.

"Yeh, Will, do you fancy the club tonight, then? I'm not really dressed for it but we could go for a while."

"Let's do it, then."

"I'm just going to get some water, back in a min." Suddenly thirsty I asked for a pint glass of tap water and took a few slugs. I turned my head towards the MI5 couple, hoping they would see me. Ginny did, and our eyes locked for a few seconds before she quickly put her head down.

No, Ginny, no, you're not getting away with that, I thought. I had to make her acknowledge me and there was only one way to do it. No words, they would be wasted on her. I moved slowly across the sticky carpet towards their table and put my glass down in front of her. She looked up, and I swear she squirmed in her seat. I gave her a nice, sweet smile and held her gaze as with one finger I tipped my drink towards her. The glass clattered on the table and rolled away but not before it had emptied its cold contents into her lap. She stood up sharply brushing herself down and gasping and flapping her arms.

I heard her spluttering, trying to say something but trying not to speak to me at the same time. It was pathetic.

"Will, let's go," I instructed as I grabbed my jacket and headed for the door. Will had watched the scene unfold and we ducked out of the pub, chuckling together.

In the car as we drove towards the pier Will asked why exactly, all those months ago, had I decided to go back to the religion anyway.

"You were free of it all, you'd starting building your own life and making new friends and you seemed happy enough. What possessed you to get tied up with it again?"

"You know why I went back. It was Ray's death. I needed something comforting and something to believe in again. Some spirituality in my life."

"And looking back now do you think you found it?"

"To some degree, yes, I think so. Let's not get into this now, Will. Can we talk about it tomorrow? I want to get dancing. D'you think any of the others will be there tonight?"

"Let's see."

A few familiar faces showed themselves and, for a spur of the moment decision, it turned out to be a good night. I kept my head and didn't have too much to drink but this time it was out of choice rather than because I had a meeting to go to the next morning. It was good to be back.

The postman woke me up with his clattering of the letterbox. The first post usually arrived about 7.30am and I sometimes caught him just as I was leaving for work. Today he shoved a single white envelope into my hand and I knew immediately who it was from. I stuffed it in my bag. I'd read it later after work. Not that I didn't want to hear from mum but I couldn't risk having my whole day spoiled and not be able to keep my mind on my work. No, mum, you'll have to wait.

Sandy was being very helpful at work. I occasionally got stuck on the new tasks I'd been set and she was the one I went to for advice.

"Good to see you looking more like your old self these days," she remarked. "You coming round for dinner tonight?"

"Er, yeh, yeh, why not."

"It won't be anything special, pie and mash, something like that."

"Well, that's fine by me." Just like old times. My going back to the meetings had affected, but not damaged I'm grateful to say, my relationships with Sandy and Ellie. They were still the same bubbly pair as they always were, reassuringly completely bonkers and I wouldn't be without them.

As I lay in bed after an evening of steak and kidney and laughter with the girls my mind returned to the issue Will had raised yesterday. I'd observed a shift in attitude amongst some of the Witnesses since I'd been back, not least my own.

I recalled several times whilst out on the ministry when the "national average" was mentioned. Mutterings of having to stay out on the ministry on freezing cold days just so they can match the national average of 12 hours a month. A personal goal maybe, and there's nothing wrong in aiming for a target, but surely going from door to door was a personal thing. The pressure was on and an air of competition had sprung up. Personally, I resented every time I submitted a monthly report stating how many hours I'd done and the number of magazines and books I'd placed. It felt wrong to keep such a score, as if it was a business exercise. And all so the Organisation could boast in the next Yearbook about how the Witnesses are the only ones preaching the good news of God's Kingdom and, 'just look how many hours we spend doing just that!'

One or two of the younger ones were reaching out for privileges within the congregation – to be assigned a role on the Quick Build Team or to be accepted as a Regular Pioneer, and all of a sudden the number of times they stuck their hand up and made a comment increased. Their answers were exemplary with scripture references and quotes from past magazines. Showing off or making spiritual progress? A means to an end? I shouldn't judge them, really. It just didn't feel right. And now, looking back, I could see just how far my own focus had shifted.

Since going back to the meetings, what I did in a spiritual way, I'd started to do for the Elders. Not for God. I needed to be observed by the Elders doing what was required to be viewed as a good Jehovah's Witness: meetings, ministry, answering up, being kind and loving to others, the whole shebang. But equally, as I went about my daily life, with or without Will, I needed *not* to be spotted by them doing something or being somewhere I shouldn't, such as tottering my way down to Dixieland or at the counter in WH Smith's with a fistful of Christmas cards. That beautiful necklace that Esther had given me for my birthday was still in its box and hadn't seen the light of day. Fearful that I would accidently go to a meeting with it still hanging round my neck I never wore it. Couldn't risk being seen wearing it.

I realised I had turned into a people-pleaser, and I felt disgusted with myself.

And here I stood, back in the same position I'd been in before, cut off and alone with the only way to get my family back being to become that people-pleaser again. Where was my faith? Did I still want to worship God? Put the Kingdom first in my life? I still couldn't answer these questions, but one thing was for certain: the only thing that would keep me going to the meetings long enough to be reinstated was this – the utter desperation to be with my family and friends again. Not to please God. I realised I wasn't doing it for Him any longer. How could that be right?

And yet, this was what the Organisation had created. It was like having a gun pointed at my head; if you don't do this you will never see your family again. It was nothing short of emotional blackmail. And the saddest thing was that I wasn't the only one this had happened to. The time I went round to Kathy's to research new years' celebrations, I'd spotted an article entitled: "Breathing This World's "Air" Is Death-Dealing!" It asked the question: "How had Jehovah's people been affected by this "air" or worldly spirit?" The answer was shocking. It went on: "Unfortunately, during the 1986 service year, 37,426 had to be disfellowshipped from the Christian congregation, the greater number of them for practicing sexual immorality."**

That's 37,426 families destroyed. A huge number of former baptised Witnesses suffering isolation, depression, stress and anxiety. Part of me had wanted to search for the same statistics from other years but there wasn't time. In any case, it was too distressing to see such figures, knowing that my friend Alan, would have been among them, and, of course, myself, back in 1984.

Petra shuffled her way into the bedroom, sniffing in my bag at the half-bar of chocolate in the side pocket. I suppose it was time to read mum's letter. I steeled myself for a thorough blasting off, to be called selfish and weak but the tone of mum's few words actually surprised me.

Dear Jessica,

Thank you for your letter. Kathy had already phoned me about you being disfellowshipped but I appreciate you letting me know yourself. I could see this happening and, quite frankly, I thought it has to be your choice. You know what the process is so I hope you put your life in order and get yourself back in Jehovah's arms as quickly as you can. This is no time to delay. Armageddon is so close now. You know the safest place to be is within His earthly Organisation.

To answer your question about why I chose to stick with the Witnesses I will be sending you my diaries. Keep them, I don't want them. Perhaps they will help you to understand.

I look forward to seeing you when you come back. You know I won't be in touch again. Don't leave it too long.

Love mum.

No kisses.

It was better than I expected, but factual and to the point. That was mum. Straight down the line. No mention of a wedding date so I guessed she didn't want me to know. Diaries, though. I'd seen them in her personal box. She showed me once many years ago. They covered the late sixties and early seventies. As a child I'd flicked through them and could read only an odd word here and there, the problem being that they were written in shorthand.

What use would they be to me if I couldn't understand them? I'd have to find someone who understood shorthand. And there was yet another problem: mum had said she used a form of shorthand (Greg) that was only taught in Ireland, where she'd learned it, and in America. Where would I even begin to find someone who knew what those squiggles meant?

But I wanted to understand how I'd come to this point in my life, with my family having been torn apart because of this religion, and the remaining family cutting me off because of the same religion. I needed to understand mum before I could understand myself. The answers were out there, I was sure of it, but it may take some time to find them.

I showed the letter to Esther the next day and as she read it, I watched her face for her reaction. She just raised her eyebrows.

"Well, at least she replied, you've got that to be grateful for. Maybe, along with writing to Bethany you should keep writing to your mum as well. Don't just disappear, keep reminding her that you still exist."

"I'll see how it goes, Esther. Do you fancy a swim together on Saturday morning? First swim of the year?"

"Could do. A quick dip would be good. Cold, but I've seen a few swimmers in already. Better pray that wind settles down."

The wind always made the water feel colder for some reason. I started getting my swim bag ready even though Saturday was a few days away. Cossie, towel, flip flops, woolly hat. Best to keep head and hands out of the water. I didn't see myself actually, literally swimming any distance but simply to be in the water, I know, would be so refreshing. I wondered if anyone else would be brave enough to come along.

I set about making a few phone calls. Theresa said no straight away – it would be too cold for the kids. I said leave them with Neil for a couple of hours, tell him to take them to the Wimpy for breakfast. She said she'd think about it. Gail said she'd come, Sandy was sceptical and said she'd go in if someone took her hand and ran in with her. Ellie shouted down the phone that she'd be the one to do that. Dominic, surprisingly, said yes. The others including Mark and Jane from the Beefeater, with a bit of gentle persuasion, all agreed to give it a go. Dominic suggested we have a fire on the beach afterwards, and hot drinks. We should all bring a couple of pieces of wood to burn and flasks of tea. Esther said she'd make bacon rolls and everyone could get changed out of their wet things back at the house. It would be a great morning to kickstart the spring.

Saturday arrived. This was it. No bottling out now that everyone had turned up. A gentle westerly breeze was blowing – chilly but not unbearable. Swimming stuff under our clothes Esther, Will and I flip-flopped down to the beach and dumped our bags, pieces of wood from the shed and a large flask of tea in a pile. Everyone had turned up within about twenty minutes and we all stood with grins of doubt on our faces, including mine, as Will told me. This was going to be freeeezing! Nervous laughter was the only kind there was as coats, sweatshirts and track suit bottoms were discarded. Chattering teeth was the soundtrack as we formed a line, taking our neighbours' hands and squeezing tight. Ther pebbles crunched and moved under our feet as we descended towards the water, reaching the flat sand.

Will stood in the middle of the line and took charge. We all bent our knees, scrunched up our faces and prepared ourselves for the impact of the icy cold water.

"Ready, steady, GO!"

We ran at that water like it was a mountain to climb, screaming and shouting and laughing as the water touched our legs, thighs and midriffs. All we could do was dance and jump about with our hands on our heads to keep them dry.

"Get your shoulders under!" shouted Esther to anyone that could hear over the screeching.

It was so painful, like a thousand knives stabbing my skin all at the same time. And yet it was also exhilarating. I felt fully awake and in the moment as the water reached my earlobes. That was deep enough. No swimming for me, maybe next time. Sandy braved a few strokes and Dominic lay on his back for about three seconds. A few minutes was all I could stand and as I made my way back to the shore others followed behind, skipping and jumping over the waves.

Towelled off and footwear back on we ran across the stones to the house and in through the side door. Friends scattered to different parts of the house to get changed, Petra not knowing who to follow. She didn't know what was going on, poor thing, and she kept barking with all the excitement. Once we were dry and dressed Esther and I set about making the bacon rolls.

The boys, Will, Mark, Dominic and others dashed back down to the beach to get the fire started and by the time the rest of us had arrived it was burning nicely. Rolls demolished, the flasks were poured and cups cradled as we all huddled around the roaring flames. Petra nudged me and pushed herself between myself and Will.

I looked up at the sky. A shy sun was looking down upon us, and I told the wispy clouds to disappear. The chilly breeze had dropped, and the small waves had reduced to rolling laps, tickling the shoreline. It was a beautiful day and I was with beautiful people.

In my own piece of silence, I realised something. The sun actually, literally shines every day. It's just that sometimes it's hidden by the clouds. But it's always there. Like those cliffs, like the sea and the sand and the pebbles. They will be there till the end of time. Reliable and dependable. Like unconditional love.

EPILOGUE

After all that had happened, did I still believe that God existed? Yes, but that's all I could get my head around at this point. Did he love me? I still felt that he did. Had he *himself* cut me off, consigned me to destruction when he brings about Armageddon? Did God count me as such an evil person, worthy of being put to death? I didn't think so. But the Witnesses had shown me that, yes, I really was that wicked. And they'd said it twice now. Mum agreed and so did Peter and every other Witness that knows me. But something stronger than them, something deep in my heart, told me they must be wrong.

Armageddon? I would take my chances. I loved Will with all my heart and couldn't live without him. He was my life partner, my best friend, my soul mate. I didn't often pray but when I did, besides giving thanks, there was one request that I repeated more than any other. And that was this: that if marriage, in the twentieth century sense, actually made a difference to God, if it *really* mattered to him, that he would somehow let me know. Maybe I would be inundated with leaflets through the door advertising wedding dresses, or perhaps I would repeatedly stumble into a wedding party while crossing through the church grounds as I often did – I don't know. But the message would be clear and unmistakable.

The loyalty and faithfulness that Will and I have in our relationship is the important thing. And that's something worth, not dying for as the Witnesses would have it, but worth living for.

The Onward Journey

References:

*Reasoning From the Scriptures
*You Can Live Forever in Paradise on Earth
*Your Youth – Getting the Best Out of It all previously published by Watchtower, Bible and Tract Society. Now out of print.

** jw.org   Ref: w87 9/15 pp. 10-15

Further reading:

Author: *Robert Crompton*
Pathways to Freedom
Leaving Gilead

Author: *Jonny Halfhead*
The 1975 Apocalypse
Nine Pills
The Offence of Grace
God to Goth

Author: *Bonnie Zieman*
Exiting the JW Cult: A Healing Handbook for current and former Jehovah's Witnesses